THE MOMENT OF DEATH

"That's a fine dog you got, mister. Yes indeedy. I reckon it would protect its master until its last breath, just as you've said. That's why I have no choice but to do this." He pulled the pistol and shot Squatter, right there before my eyes.

"No!" I yelled. "No!"

Already Copper had picked up his hatchet and was advancing toward me. It was as if I were frozen in place, unable to move. His shooting of Squatter had stunned me into paralysis.

I broke out of it too late to dodge the blow. The hatchet went back, came forward, and pain, far more explosive and racking than that inflicted earlier by Manchester the wagoner, cracked like lightning in my head as the flat side of the hatchet struck me. I fell to my knees, then forward, landing partly atop Squatter.

He whimpered and moved beneath me. "Squatter . . ." I reached up to touch his twitching snout. Then Eb Copper appeared above me, squatting down to examine me.

"I reckon I didn't hit you hard enough," he said.

He hefted up the hatchet again. I closed my eyes and awaited the death blow. . . .

CONFEDERATE GOLD

CAMERON JUDD

BANTAM BOOKS
NEW YORK • TORONTO • LONDON • SYDNEY • AUCKLAND

CONFEDERATE GOLD
A Bantam Domain Book / December 1993

ISBN 0-553-56051-4

Published simultaneously in the United States and Canada

PRINTED IN THE UNITED STATES OF AMERICA

RAD   0 9 8 7 6 5 4 3 2 1

To the Carrigans of Portland:
Mark, Kim, Clay, and Jesse

CONFEDERATE GOLD

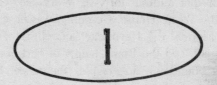

1

She looked at me through the smoke of her corncob pipe and declared she wanted me to take her home, and I never knew until the day of her death years later whether it was because of a real longing for the place of her raising or because she wanted to give me a way to get myself out of trouble.

"Home?" I said. "Fort Scott *is* home. It's where we make our living. It's where we buried Pap."

"My home is Tennessee," my mother replied. "The living we make here ain't much, and I'm pining for the hills. I want to go back to Rogersville and live with your aunt Kate. I want you to take me."

"It's because of the fight, ain't it!" I said. "You're trying to get me away from here to keep me out of jail."

She leaned forward, that blue glint of her eyes as keen as the flash of a new gun barrel. "Enoch Brand, you ain't never talked back to your mother in twenty-five years of life, and I don't expect you to start now. There's a Tennessee-bound wagon train going to be

1

pulling out soon. We'll be a part of it. I want you to take me home, and there's no more to be said about it."

And that's all that was said about it, and how it all began in that autumn forty-six years ago. Cleveland was in the White House, Geronimo was on a reservation in Florida, the Haymarket anarchists of Chicago were in jail, and the Brand family of Fort Scott, Kansas, was bound for Rogersville, Tennessee, the little town from which we had sprung. That was how Prudence Brand had said it would be, and there was no arguing with her.

The truth was, I was grateful. I needed to get away from Fort Scott as quickly as possible, or find myself in jail for beating Hermes Van Horn half to death. That was the deal I had been offered by the court, but until Ma declared her desire to leave, I hadn't been able to accept it, and my time to choose was running out fast.

I hadn't meant to hurt Hermes so bad. But it was his fault as much as mine, for he had flirted with Minnie, my dear wife, one time too many. A man can only abide so much of that, even when, to be honest, the wife is doing as much of the flirting as the other party.

Minnie had a way of drawing men; I should know, for she had drawn me all the way to the church altar. The trouble was, her attractiveness didn't fade after my ring went around her finger. Men flocked to her like roosters to a hen, and she made little effort to spur them off. It was a vexing thing to endure. I guess that's why I was so rough on Hermes Van Horn when finally I had put up with enough of his lechery: I was unloading on him the full weight of vexation that had been building for a long time.

Minnie hadn't always been an unfaithful-hearted wife. At the beginning of our marriage she was as true as a woman could be. And then had come the great tragedy of her life, one that had jolted her to the heart and left her changed. Nobody ever really knew what happened to bring it about, but the short of it was that her mother was killed. Murdered by shotgun—and the one who did it was Minnie's father, who turned the second barrel on himself when his wife was dead. He had always drunk too much, so much it had gone to his liver and maybe his brain as well. That was how I account for what he did, but like I say, nobody ever really knew.

The murder sent Minnie into a month-long silence. It was like her form was present but her soul was way off somewhere else. And after she came out of it, she was different than the Minnie I had known. The flirting started, the too-long glances at other men, the moodiness, the seeming inability for her to decide whether she really loved me or not. I didn't hold her to fault for it; how could I, knowing what she had gone through? How could I ever think of raising my voice, much less my hand, against a woman who had seen her own mother murdered by her father? Minnie's suffering had changed me as much as it had changed her. It had made me love her more deeply than ever, and given me a world of patience with her trying ways. Maybe too much patience; after you hear my story, you can decide that for yourself.

Of course, a man can grow frustrated in being patient, and frustration can boil over into fury, as it had with Hermes Van Horn. All the anger I had been un-willing to take out on Minnie I took out on him.

And so now I had to leave, and Ma's declaration gave me the perfect opportunity to do it. In a way, the move would be relatively easy. We were a poor family, always had been, so there were few goods that would have to be carried along to Tennessee. Mostly just some of Ma's old furniture and quilts and other such things that are the treasures of aging widows. Beyond that there were the household goods Minnie and I possessed, and few these were, for we had shared the little rented house at Fort Scott with Ma, and there had been scant room for accumulation.

I would leave behind my smithy fixings, my anvil, hammers, bellows, tongs, and so on, and have them sold. I was a blacksmith in those days, like my father before me had been, and I was good at it, even though I seemed perpetually unable to make a decent living at the forge.

The day after Ma declared our destiny, I set about getting ready to leave. Minnie didn't like the idea at all. She was a Kansan and had never been out of her home state, except to cross the line a few miles into Missouri. She cried and fussed half the night after I told her we were leaving, but this did her no good. She cried and fussed all the time anyway, so I had grown deaf to her complaints.

What would happen soon after would make me realize that perhaps I should have listened to Minnie more than I did. I would find that not even Prudence Brand could lay out a destiny unalterable by circumstance and a wayward woman. Before this adventure was done, I would find myself not rolling back into Tennessee as anticipated, but deep in the hills of Arkansas, searching for my woman, fighting my way through troubles far worse than those I was fleeing, and following the dangerous path of a strange and obsessed man whose life was wrapped up in a lost strongbox of Confederate gold. But I'm getting ahead of my story.

There were two other families bound for Tennessee from Fort Scott at that time. As bad luck would have it, one of them was the Malan clan, fathered by Bert Malan, uncle-by-marriage of Hermes Van Horn. Bert and I had always gotten along tolerably up until my row with Hermes. After that, however, I could all but smell the bad blood running through his veins every time I got near him.

Only his respect for my mother had led Bert Malan to let us become part of the wagon train at all. I decided to stay as clear of him as possible for the sake of group harmony, and devote my attention solely to driving the wagon, helping Ma with the cooking along the way (Minnie being a sorry cook who complained about the job so much that she usually escaped it), and generally looking out for trouble. There didn't seem much possibility of the latter. After all, this was 1886, modern times, and we would be traveling in settled territory all the way.

Our route would be from Fort Scott to Carthage, Missouri, on to Springfield, across the plateau of the Ozarks to Cape Girardeau, across the river and on into Mound City, Kentucky, then to Paducah, Hopkinsville, Guthery, and into Tennessee about Gallatin. From there we would travel across the midst of the state, over the Cumberland Plateau, into East Tennessee and Knoxville, the stopping point for the rest of the travelers. My family would head on northeast from there, to the old homeplace at Rogersville.

There was no sadness on my part when it came time to roll out of Fort Scott on our big covered wagons. Ma might have felt sad to leave behind the place where she had laid to rest her husband; if so, she hid it, as she always hid her feelings. As for Minnie, she was weepy and maudlin, wiping her tears and nose on the cuff of her jacket, an old castoff of mine that fit her like a tent.

The horses, belonging to a blacksmithing family, were already well-shod. Our two wagons weren't as well off and required quite a bit of repair. By the day of our departure, however, they were in as good a shape as old vehicles could be. The axles were greased, loose sideboards tightened, brakes checked and repaired. Loading followed a sensible pattern, with goods such as skillets and pots, along with foodstuffs, packed on top of those things that would not be required for use during the journey. The canvas that was stretched across the bows was new and unpunctured.

Hermes Van Horn came to see off his kin, and maybe to make sure I was really leaving. I walked up to him, stuck out my hand, and tried not to stare too much at the bruises I had left blotching his face. His round head, marked with the dark impressions of my fist, reminded me of one of those world globes you often see in schoolhouses.

"Hermes, I'm sorry we are parting on bad terms," I said. "I might have liked you if you could have just left Minnie alone."

He looked at my extended hand like it held something scooped from the floor of a chicken coop. Without a word he turned away from me, snorting derisively, and stomped off.

Bert Malan came up to me, a gruff look on his face. "You trying to pick a fight again, Brand? You stay clear of him, and of me too, if you know what's good for you. It ain't out of love for you that I've agreed to let you come along, you know."

"Just trying to make up for past hurts, Bert," I replied, and turned back to my wagon. All I had tried to do was be a peacemaker, and even though my effort had been spurned, I felt then and forever thereafter that I had done the right thing to try.

The caravan set off with a creak and a groan. Minnie was overcome with emotion and crawled back under the bows and canvas to bury herself among the bundles and strapped-down furniture. There she cried, peering out through the back opening. I don't know what she saw in Kansas that was so all-fired hard to give up. Her own parents were dead and her brothers and sisters well-scattered across the country. I had to wonder if it was Hermes Van Horn she was grieving for. Thinking about that made me mad.

Our family brought up the rear of the caravan, with me driving the final wagon. The one ahead, carrying Ma, was driven by a twenty-year-old member of the Malan family, Joseph Benjamin Malan, whose double name had been shortened down and slurred together for so long that he now went by "Joben." He even spelled it that way, perhaps because he thought doing so was cute and clever, or more likely because he was too stupid to know Joben wasn't a real name.

And stupid he was—one of the worst cases I've ever seen then or since. Joben Malan hadn't made it through the first year of school and couldn't count past twenty without getting crossed up. Even his family considered him an idiot. And lest it appear that I am overharsh in my description of Joben because of what happened between him and Minnie soon thereafter, let me balance things by noting that he was as handsome a man as one would ever meet. He was tall, dark-haired, friendly, and muscular, possessing many qualities women find appealing in a man. My own Minnie, it turned out, was one of those women.

Traveling in the wagon with Minnie and me was Minnie's parrot, a gift to her from one of her brothers the previous Christmas. Minnie, not a very imaginative woman, had given it the name Bird. It was quite a creature, capable of repeating almost anything it heard. Ma had even managed to teach it the first two lines of an Isaac Watts hymn. Minnie was only mildly fond of the bird; Ma like it a little better but found its chatter hard on the nerves.

My big hound, Squatter, ambled along beside the wagon. He had been my companion since I got him as a pup, and he was a beloved beast. He was strong, easygoing, and a good watchdog, and best of all, loyal. And a man with a wife like Minnie needed loyalty, if only from his hound.

The first day's travel, southward and east, went well. The weather was clear and fine, the road smooth. The more miles that piled up between me and Fort Scott, the better I felt. Maybe back in Tennessee, the home of my youth, I could make a better go of it than I had in Kansas.

We camped that night at Carthage, Missouri, right on schedule. It had been a long day's haul, right at fifty miles, and both beasts and humans were weary. The site of our camp was good, rich with wood and water, and Ma built a roaring fire. After a supper consisting of numerous bowls of soup, I finished the final chores of the day's end and settled back with a pipe. Ma had her pipe out too, and was puffing quite contently. Squatter was sleeping beside her, making her warm and comfortable.

Fifteen or so minutes later I noticed that Minnie wasn't about. I asked Ma, who said she had seen Minnie walking across the camp, up toward where Bert Malan and his kin were encamped. I waited around a little longer for Minnie to return, and she didn't. At last I began to worry for her, and decided to go find her, even if it did mean going where I wasn't welcome.

Bert Malan saw me coming and stood. "What do you want, Brand?"

"I'm looking for Minnie. You seen her?"

"What's that supposed to mean? You implying something?"

"It means I haven't see Minnie in a while, and Ma says she had come over this way. That's what it means, and that's all it means." I swear, this man was aggravating enough to make the Pope cuss.

Joben Malan stood. He had a cup of hot coffee in a tin mug, and instead of holding it by the handle, he was cupping it with his fingers, shifting it to the other hand when it burned him, then shifting it back again when the second hand got too hot. So you can see it's not simple meanness on my part when I say he was stupid.

"I seen her," Joben said. "She was heading for the woods yonder."

"When was that?"

"A good hour ago, I'd say." He looked off in the

direction Minnie had gone, and on his good-looking face was a deeply wistful, longing expression. That expression should have forewarned me of troubles to come. "I reckon she'd have hollered if something was wrong. And I'd have been proud to help her if she had, Enoch. I ain't got nothing against you, not me."

And right then, as if Joben's words had triggered it, Minnie's screech came ringing out from the woods. It brought everyone in the camp to their feet, and sent me scampering. Joben followed, along with Bert and two or three others.

Minnie came racing out of the woods and right into my arms. "He's terrible, he's just terrible!" she yelled. Her face was streaked with tears and she was even more distraught than I was used to seeing her.

"Who's terrible?"

No answer was required, because the man in reference came striding out of the woods right then. It was Dewey Manchester, a hired hand of Bert Malan and driver of one of his three wagons. I hardly knew Manchester, but I did know his reputation. He was a troublemaker and had thrice gotten himself in hot water by acting in unseemly ways toward Fort Scott women. A man had knifed Manchester across the face for pawing his wife once upon a time, and the scar was broad and ugly and only partially hidden by his beard.

"What were you doing back there with my wife?" I demanded.

It was dark, but there was enough moonlight to let me see his maddening grin. "I took me a stroll at the same time she did, that's all. I didn't even know she was there until I stumbled upon her."

"He was watching me!" Minnie said. "I turned around and there he was, and he grabbed at me too!"

She held up her arm. "See that scratch? It was his fingernail that done it!"

"Manchester, I'll peel your hide like a pelt if what she's saying is true!" It was a poor choice of words, for Minnie pulled away and looked at me angrily.

"*If* it's true? Of course it's true—you think I'd lie?"

"I'm sorry, Minnie, that's not what I meant."

"I never touched her," Manchester said. He had a cool, smug manner that made me want to light into him right there.

Bert Malan stepped between me and Manchester. "Whatever happened, there's nobody hurt and no reason for this to go on any longer," he said. "Enoch Brand, I suggest you get back to your wagon, and keep a closer watch on your wife."

That made me mad and got the best of my hard-pressed restraint. "Bert Malan, you're treading a narrow log. You'd best watch your step, or you might take a tumble right off it."

He lifted a finger and pointed it in my face, squinting down its length like it was a pistol barrel. "It's you who'd best watch your step, Brand. I'm the boss of this train, and I'll throw you off it quicker than you can scratch your backside"—he glanced at the several women present—"your nose. Quicker than you can scratch your nose."

Joben Malan edged up to Minnie. "Are you all right, ma'am?"

She looked at him like she had just noticed his looks for the first time. Like a storybook princess would look at the knight who just saved her. Like Squatter would look at a fresh beefsteak.

"Why, thank you, Joben Malan," she said. Her

voice was suddenly a soft, cooing thing, almost musical. It was painful to me to hear it. She hadn't used that voice with me for the longest time.

At that moment Squatter came rushing up. He had stayed back at the fireside with Ma, but had been drawn by the excitement. He must have sensed my hostility toward Manchester, for he snarled and would have leaped on him had I not reached down and grabbed him by his rope collar at the last second.

"That's it—this little gathering is finished," Bert Malan said. "Get on back to your place, Brand, and keep that mastiff away from good folk before it hurts somebody."

I might have spoken my mind to Bert Malan right then if not for my sense that this whole thing was about to get beyond control. With a great effort of will I swallowed my angry words and backed off. "Come on, Squatter," I said. "Come on, Minnie."

"I'm glad you're all right, Mrs. Brand," Joben said. He hadn't looked at me once, just stared at her with a dreamy gaze.

"Thank you, Joben," Minnie said. "You're quite a gentleman."

As we walked together back toward our camp, I asked her what had possessed her to take a stroll into the woods at such an odd time.

"Maybe you ain't noticed, but there's no privies in this camp," she replied.

"Oh."

We went a little farther. "You sure were acting awfully sweet toward Joben back there."

"He's a gentleman. A woman acts kind to gentlemen."

"Are you saying I'm not one?"

"What are you fussing on me so hard for?" She began to act upset, her voice rising. "You're always fussing on me, Enoch. I try to be a good wife, and you just fuss!"

"Don't talk so loud—folks are looking."

"I don't care! Let them look! Let them see a husband dragging his wife off from her home against her will, and see what they think of that!"

I said no more, out of fear of public humiliation. We reached our campsite, and I found myself thinking it was going to be one dreadfully long and trying trip before we made it all the way to Rogersville.

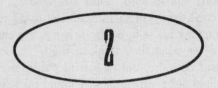

2

The first night of the journey had taken a bad turn, but I was optimistic enough to hope matters would improve afterward. Instead they only worsened the next day.

Bert Malan despise me more than ever and made no efforts to hide his feelings. For the sake of my mother and wife, I tried to ignore him. He made that difficult, talking about me to the rest of the travelers, calling me a troublemaker who had wrongly beaten his nephew, saying I would have been a murderer if someone hadn't restrained me when I was pounding on Hermes Van Horn. That, more than any other of his words, made me furious, because it wasn't true. Certainly I had given Hermes a severe beating, but at no time would I have lost control to the point of killing him. Blacksmithing had given me much physical strength; I knew the danger of unleashing it, and always kept it in sufficient check. So far, at least.

Minnie also continued to make the journey difficult. Obviously she had become smitten with Joben Malan, and all day, as she sat beside me on the wagon seat, she craned her neck this way and that to catch a glimpse of him on the wagon ahead of us. When I would ask her what she was doing, she would reply that she was merely stretching her back, because it was sore from sleeping on the ground.

Joben was equally taken with Minnie, but had the decency to avoid being too open in his attentions. Of all the Malan family, Joben was the only one who didn't seem down on me because of what had happened in Fort Scott. I might have come to appreciate him for that if only he could have kept his eyes off Minnie. Try as he would, he couldn't. I would catch them glancing meaningfully at each other at odd times, and whenever Joben noticed that I had noticed, he would look the other way. Minnie didn't even bother to do that, and it caused me plenty of pain.

Even so, it wasn't Joben Malan who caused me the most concern. It was Manchester, the wagoneer. Like Joben, he was taken with Minnie, but in a way that was obviously more base and dangerous. He had no shame about it, and even seemed to enjoy stirring me up by staring openly at Minnie, and never faltering under my angry responsive glare. He came around close every time the wagons stopped for anything, and when he did, Minnie would draw up close beside me, more for protection than from affection, I suppose. Manchester scared her. He was a frightening man, to be sure. There were rumors that he had once murdered a horse trader in Ohio.

Ma saw the trouble coming even before I did. "We should get out of this wagon train," she told me. "We can go on alone. If we don't, you'll find yourself more trouble."

"I'm a grown man, Ma," I responded. "There's safety in a group. Don't worry. I'll watch my temper."

"Squatter! Here, boy! Here, Squatter!" The voice was high and harsh, and it punctuated its words with whistles.

Squatter made a throaty noise and lifted his head. I sat up. "Shut up, Bird," I said to the squawking parrot. "It's the durn middle of the night."

"Squatter! Here, boy!"

The wind had blown the cloth off the parrot's cage. I replaced it and tied the corners to the thin cage bars to ensure it stayed in place. Then I rolled over to see if the bird had awakened Minnie.

But there was no Minnie there. Her place was empty, the blankets tossed aside.

Squatter was up on his haunches. He looked east, stood, and growled into the dark. Ma was snoring in her bedroll near the fire, oblivious to the world.

I rose. Being in a mixed camp, I had worn my trousers to bed. Throwing my shirt and coat on took only a few seconds, and then I invested a few more in strapping my Colt-bearing gun belt around my waist. I had a bad feeling about this, and worried for Minnie.

The camp was a dark place of banked fires and snoring people. Squatter led me east; he had obviously detected something in that direction. Maybe just a stray dog on the perimeter of the camp. Or maybe Minnie, God forbid, snatched away by Manchester? But no; surely not. Squatter would have sent up a howl if Manchester had come around our wagon. He despised the man as much as I did.

But he didn't despise Joben. Squatter had always

liked Joben Malan, and never even sent up a growl when he was near.

I heard them before I saw them. They were on the far side of a little stand of trees and brush. It *was* Joben there with Minnie; I knew it because her voice had that cooing quality, the one she once had reserved for me.

A great fury rose inside me. My insides felt like a pot on hot boil. I wouldn't abide this. I had beaten Joben's cousin back in Fort Scott. Now I would give the same to Joben, and if it sent me to jail, to jail I'd go.

I stopped, took a deep breath, and forced myself to unbuckle my gun belt. If my temper got the best of me, I didn't want a pistol anywhere handy. I hung the belt over the stub of a branch. Clenching and unclenching my fists in anticipation, I began my advance.

And stopped it as quickly. Joben had just said something that threw the whole situation into a new and more grim light.

"You? What are *you* doing here?" I knew from his tone and the direction toward which he spoke that he wasn't addressing me. Right then, Minnie went, "Oh, no, oh, no!" and I knew that whoever they had seen was quite likely to be Manchester.

"Hello, Joben," another male voice said. I was right; it was Manchester. "What are you doing out here, cuddled up with the wife of another man?"

"You get out of here, Dewey Manchester. You was fired today and there's no cause for you to stay around."

Manchester had been fired? I hadn't heard about that. Of course, the Malans wouldn't have been likely to come running to me with the latest news. Who had fired him? It surely had been Bert Malan. No one else would have had the authority.

"I ain't never been fired until this day," Manchester said. "You want to know something, Joben? I don't like being fired. It ain't a good feeling." There was a pause, during which Manchester must have gestured toward Minnie. "Now, that right there, that's what gives a man a good feeling. But it looks like you already know that, huh?"

Joben said, "It was just that sort of trash-talk that got you fired, Dewey. Now get out of here before I have to work you over."

Manchester laughed. "You, work me over? Pshaw!" He spat on the ground. "You couldn't whip my granny, Joben. Hey now, what do you reckon your daddy would have to say about his own boy out pawing around on the wife of another man, the very day he fired his best hand over a lot less than that? What do you reckon?"

"Joben, I'm going back to the wagon," Minnie said.

And all at once it all broke loose. I couldn't see them from where I was, and so didn't know what set it off, but suddenly Minnie screamed, Joben yelled, and there was a loud scuffling. Manchester was cussing fiercely, and fists pounded flesh. I felt sure the fists were Manchester's, the flesh Joben's.

Until then I had been transfixed in my tracks, overwhelmed by a sick feeling inside that had sapped the strength from my anger. I broke out of it, grabbed and the gun belt off the branch and vaulted toward the fighters, breaking into the clearing at the same moment I got the pistol out of the holster. I flung the empty gun belt aside. Squatter snarled, barked, and flashed past me. He had been waiting for me to move; now that I had, he was in the fight even before I could reach it.

I could tell from some muffled, chopped-off words that burst out of Joben that Manchester had a pistol. Something moved in the air; a terrible, metal-against-bone thud informed me that Manchester had just connected his swung pistol with Joben's skull. Joben fell. Minnie screamed and ran off into the dark. Squatter threw his big form against Manchester and had the bad luck to have his own skull struck by Manchester's big pistol. I couldn't see the weapon clearly, but figured it was surely the big, outdated Army Colt that he usually bore.

Manchester's pistol roared. In the brief lightning flash of its explosion, I saw Joben lying off to the side, Squatter collapsing at Manchester's feet, and Manchester's twisted face looking down toward the dog. It was Squatter, not Joben, who he was trying to kill.

"No!" I yelled hoarsely. Then I was against Manchester, knocking him down, landing atop him and forcing a curse and burst of stinking breath from him. His smoking pistol hit me in the side of the head. I rolled off, came to my feet in a spasmodic motion and swung my own Colt blindly.

He grunted and jerked and fell away from me. My head suddenly began to swim, as if the blow he had landed on me had taken a delayed effect. Groaning, I passed out as I heard shouts and yells from the camp.

One of the last thoughts that went through my mind was the desperate hope that Manchester's shot had somehow managed to miss Squatter. I loved that dog dearly. I didn't want him to die, especially at the hands of a man who was hardly more than a dog himself.

Then I had one more thought as the last of consciousness faded: I might not wake up again. While I was out, there would be nothing to keep Dewey Manchester from killing me—and he was just the kind of man to do it.

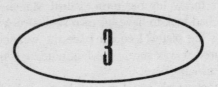

3

Minnie's tearstained face was before me when I came to. It wore a look of sincere concern that touched me, even through the clouds around my brain. To be cared about by Minnie, to have her fret over me like she had in our first days—that was all I could ask. I hungered for her affection, would have paid any price for her to feel about me as I felt about her.

"Enoch, you're alive! Oh, I'm so glad!" She bent over and hugged me. My head throbbed as she jarred me, but I smiled anyway.

Looking at me across her shoulder was another face, this one showing nothing but anger. It was Bert Malan's. The fire lit his countenance but couldn't erase the darkness of his expression as he glowered at me. Flicking my eyes around, I saw that I had been moved back to the main camp and placed within the circle of yellow cast by the fire. Across from me lay another person. Joben. He apparently was out cold ... or dead.

"Move aside, woman," Malan said to Minnie, putting his hand on her shoulder and rather roughly pushing her to the left. She rose and backed away, then went over to where Joben lay.

"Easy . . . on my wife," I said in the loudest voice I could achieve, and that was almost a whisper.

"Your wife is in just about as much trouble as you are, Enoch Brand," Bert Malan said. "I knew I shouldn't have let you into this caravan. My best judgment was against it, and if not for your mother, I'd have never done it. Well, this is what comes of not following my own good sense."

"Manchester . . . where did he go?"

"Manchester? He's long gone. I sent him packing today, the sorry lecher. But you've got worries enough of your own without bringing him into this, Brand. If Joben dies, I'll see you hang for murder."

I tried to sit up. Even as foggy as my thinking was, I could see that a great misunderstanding was under way here. "Wait a minute, Bert. It wasn't me who hit your son. It was Manchester."

"Do tell? Did he use your pistol to do it? There's blood crusting the sight. And Joben's head is laid open."

"Manchester hit Joben. I hit Manchester."

"Did you? Then where is he?"

"He ran off, I reckon. I'm just happy he didn't kill me."

"He was never here, and you know it. You'll not lie your way out of this one."

Hot breath hit my face, then a wet canine tongue licked my cheek. "Squatter! You're alive!"

"Get that hound away from here," Bert instructed a man standing nearby. The man advanced. Squatter snarled and growled deep in his throat. The man glanced at Malan, shook his head and backed off.

"Why did you do it, Enoch? Why did you hurt Joben?"

"I didn't . . . I told you, it was Manchester."

Bert knelt and spoke so others around couldn't hear. "Listen, Brand—I know Joben has been smit with your wife, and I know that he shouldn't have let himself get that way. But the truth is, that woman of yours is mighty . . . common in her ways, to put it the nicest way possible. She led him on. Tell the truth— you came out here to kill him, didn't you?"

Rising anger was giving me my fortitude again. "I came out here because I woke up and found Minnie gone from beside me. I was afraid somebody had come and dragged her off."

"What? With that big hound of yours guarding your spot? You ask me to believe that story?"

"I figured it was Joben—Squatter never barks at Joben. And I was right. But Manchester showed up before I could get to them. He and Joben fought, and I came in when Joben got knocked down. Manchester hit Squatter too, and shot at him. I managed to pistol-whip Manchester; it's his blood that's on my pistol sight, not Joben's."

"Your pistol also has an empty shell in it. It was you who fired that shot, not Manchester. And you were shooting at Joben. Admit it!"

"No. Because it's not true. That empty has been in my pistol for three days."

Joben groaned. Minnie yelled out, "Glory be! He's come back to us!" and hugged Joben just like she had hugged me earlier, only this hug was more enthu-siastic.

Joben moaned in a trembling voice, tried to sit up and failed. Minnie said, "Joben, are you all right?"

The big oaf looked up at her with the blankest of faces and spoke words that evidenced the blankest of minds. "Mama, is that you? Mama, I fell out of the tree!"

Lord help us, I thought. He was fool enough before, and now he's worse.

"Joben, it's me, Minnie!"

"Mama, help me to the outhouse. Hurry, or I won't make it!"

"Well, he's too addled to clarify anything you've said," Bert said.

"Then ask Minnie."

"Her word means nothing. She'd naturally cover for her husband."

Someone stepped up beside me. I looked up and saw Ma's prunish face. Her pipe was clamped between her teeth and she wore a harsh expression.

"Mr. Malan, I don't like the way you're talking to my son," she said.

Malan faced her. "I hope you'll understand, Mrs. Brand. Enoch has injured Joben, just like he injured my nephew Hermes in Fort Scott. I have no choice but to be harsh with him."

"Can you prove he did this?" She waved at Joben, who was still addle-brained and urging "Mama" to take him to the outhouse. A pause, and then he said, very despairingly, "Too late! Too late! I tried to tell you, Mama, but you wouldn't listen!"

Bert Malan ignored his son, around whom everyone was suddenly clearing a wide circle. Even Minnie had backed away. "There's evidence on Enoch's pistol that your son hit Joben," Bert said. "Mrs. Brand, I'm afraid I'm going to have to throw your son and his wife out of this wagon train. You, however, are welcome to stay. I'll have some of the boys drive your wagons."

"Don't believe I want to stay in a train led by a man who's been looking for any bad thing he can find on my boy," she said.

"I'm trying to be fair."

"Pshaw! I heard Enoch saying that your wagoner was the one who hit your son. But you don't appear too interested in checking to see if that is true."

"I'll be straightforward with you, Mrs. Brand: I don't want that daughter-in-law of yours around to entice my boy into doing wrong things."

"Hah! So now we're getting more to the truth! You think my boy and his wife to be so much rubbish! You just been looking for a way to get shut of them, ain't you!"

"I'm sorry you don't understand, Mrs. Brand," he said.

"You must admit that your younger kin have caused a lion's share of trouble for me and mine."

I had managed to sit up by now. "Don't argue with him, Ma. Let him throw me off," I said. "I can follow on later."

"I won't hear of such as that," she said.

"Well, this can be took up come daylight," Bert said. "At the moment, we should all return to our sleeping places and get what rest we can."

Ma was ready to argue with him, but I reached out and touched her hand. "Let it go, Ma. He's been looking for the chance to do this anyway. It's for the best; if I stay on, there'll be nothing but more trouble."

We went back to the wagon, but slept no more

that night. I argued with Ma about the idea of me and Minnie leaving, until at last I had persuaded her not to fight the notion. Furthermore, I convinced her to remain with the wagon train, which could provide her more company and safety than I could alone.

I also had an ulterior motive for keeping Ma in the caravan. I wanted the chance to be alone with Minnie, to try once and for all to win her affections again. That would be hard to do with a third person close by.

It angered me that I would not be given the chance to prove that Manchester, not me, was responsible for hurting Joben. But what did it matter, really? Bert Malan was determined to think the worst of me, no matter what the truth was. I was just glad nobody had been killed in the nocturnal fight, and that I wasn't going to have to put up with Malan any longer. Let the wagon train go on ahead; I could follow a day or so behind, and meet up with Ma in Knoxville.

That is, if Minnie would be cooperative. She was a miserable woman at the moment. She had just realized that she was about to become an outcast, and grieved over it like she had been sentenced to death. When she wandered off again, telling me she wanted to be alone, I didn't follow her, even though I knew that most likely "alone" meant being with Joben Malan once more.

We were put off with a couple of riding horses and one packhorse, my Colt pistol and aging but well-kept Henry rifle, food, blankets, clothing, and sundry other items that would see us through as we followed the wagon train. There was Squatter too, and Bird the parrot. Ma didn't want to have to put up with its chatter across three states, so I had agreed to keep him with us.

It really wasn't so much a case of Minnie and I leaving the wagon train as the train leaving us. We simply remained in camp while the wagons rolled out. It was sad to see Ma looking back around the canvas, watching us recede from her sight.

"It's just as well, I reckon," I told Minnie. "My head aches something fierce from where Manchester clouted me. I could use a day or so of rest. Besides, Minnie, it's a chance for us to be together."

She smiled at me, but it was a sad sort of smile. Lord knows that woman knew how to make me feel melancholy to the bottom of my soul.

It was odd, but I slept most of the next day. I say it was odd because I've always been a light sleeper, getting by on five or so hours of sleep a night. I suppose it had to do with the blow to the head that I had suffered.

Minnie moped around most of the day, and often I caught her wistfully looking off in the direction the caravan had taken. Most likely she was thinking of Joben.

On the second day I felt much more fit, and we traveled, following the tracks of the wagons. That night we camped on the edge of Springfield, apparently again on the same place the wagon train had put up a night earlier. I judged this based on the dead fires, tracks, tramped earth and such.

"I want to go into town, Enoch," Minnie said.

"Well, I don't blame you for that. We'll go. I might even scrape up enough money for us to have an honest-to-goodness restaurant meal. What do you think of that?"

"I'd like that," she said, and gave me a smile, a real one, not one of her fakes. I was encouraged.

That night in Springfield, dining with Minnie in a restaurant on meager money I had no business spending, was one of the best evenings of my life. I hardly cared right then about the trouble back in Fort Scott, or the subsequent trouble over Manchester and Joben Malan. Perhaps it had all been fate, tossing us around in order to put us into a situation that would draw us closer. Minnie was as pretty a picture as I've ever seen, sitting across that table from me, drinking coffee and eating apple pie that swam in fresh cream. She insisted that we take a bottle of wine with us when we returned to camp, and once there, she poured glass after glass of it down me. Celebrating our marriage, she said.

Holding her as we fell asleep that night—passed out was more like it, in my case—I was glad she was my wife. The best part was that it seemed she was glad of it too.

She was gone the next morning. I followed her horse's tracks almost all the way back to Springfield, right up to an abandoned old livery at the edge of town. There her tracks were joined by the tracks of another horse. I recognized it as Joben Malan's, based on a funny little curl at the end of one of the horseshoes. I should recognize it; I had made the shoe myself, back in my Fort Scott smithy.

He had come sometime late in the night, while I was passed out from the wine. Had Minnie and Joben planned this mutual escape during that time she was "alone" the night before we left the train? I found my answer quickly—a wadded note at the edge of the clearing. It bore Joben's writing, and instructed Minnie to get me drunk the night we camped near Springfield, and sneak off to meet him at this old stable.

So it had been a sham. All the happiness and closeness of the previous night, that wonderful sense of togetherness in the Springfield restaurant . . . a sham.

Their tracks led south, cutting across the Ozark Plateau and toward Arkansas. Where was Joben taking her? Wherever, it was certainly away from the wagon train. Apparently he had run out on his overbearing father, who was still trying to run his life even though he was a full-grown man . . . at least in body. In brain he was still nothing but a big boy, and probably always would be.

I had mounted and was about to ride away when I heard a an odd but familiar voice. "Farleytown! Farleytown!"

"Bird?"

Indeed it was. The parrot was still in its cage, which was sitting inside the livery door. What would have possessed Minnie to bring the parrot all the way here? The best I could figure was that she had decided on a whim to take the bird wherever it was she and Joben were going, then had changed her mind once she got here and simply dumped the parrot.

"Bird, it's a good thing I found you, eh?"

"Cracker! Cracker! Cracker for the good bird! Farleytown!"

"Farleytown, eh? That's a new one. Who taught you that? Did Minnie teach you that one?"

He fluttered and shifted on his perch as I lifted the cage. "Farleytown! Farleytown!"

"Reckon she must have taught you that one, huh? I never heard of no Farleytown." I was talking at a rapid rate, trying to keep myself from being overwhelmed with sorrow. There's no more depressing thing that to wake up with a head pounding from too much wine, to find the woman you thought you had regained has been playing you for a fool, just to get away from you.

"Farleytown! Farleytown!"

I had been trudging back to my horse, but I stopped. "Wait a minute—Bird, you might have learned you a word Minnie didn't intend for you to learn! Now, wouldn't that just beat it!"

I rode into Springfield and asked the first man I met if there was a Farleytown anywhere in the region. Yes indeed, he said, though it wasn't real close. Down across the Arkansas line, south and a little westward, maybe seventy, eighty miles from where we were. I thanked him and rode back to camp. I had left Squatter guarding it, and he was glad to see me returning.

"Squatter, the inside of my head feels as ugly as your face. But I reckon I can't let that stop us, can I? We got a ride to make, and it ain't Tennessee we're bound for. We'll go back into Springfield first of all, and I'll send a letter on to Aunt Kate in Tennessee, telling her we might be a little late arriving. Minnie's run off with Joben Malan, and I believe they've gone to Arkansas. We're going to find them, and I'm going to bring Minnie back.

"Guess I'm a fool to love that gal. Lord knows she's brought us enough grief, eh?" I scratched his ears, the way he always liked it. "Better a fool than a quitter, I always say. So fools we'll just have to be. That's right, ain't it, Squatter? That's right."

I wrote the letter to Aunt Kate, asking her to send one of my cousins to meet Ma in Knoxville about the time I anticipated the wagons would get there. Then, with Squatter trotting alongside and the packhorse trailing behind, Bird's cage bobbing on its back, I rode into Springfield and posted the letter. From there we turned southwest and began to ride.

And that is how it was that in the fall of 1886 I aimed for Tennessee and wound up hitting Arkansas, the place where I would meet Leviticus Lee and first hear of the lost Confederate gold.

4

The day became grayer, the sky heavier and lower-set, the farther I advanced into the jumbled Ozark hills and mountains. Even the beauty of the autumn russets, scarlets, and yellows couldn't brighten the bloomy atmosphere. Squatter seemed as ill at ease as his master, sniffing about and growling into the woodlands as we rode.

About dusk I decided we were lost, and felt foolish for it. I had thought I could find the way to this Farleytown community—for community, rather than real town, was surely all it was. Now I wasn't all that confident. Checking the sunset, I realized I had veered off too directly westward and had managed to leave the main route.

The forest here was exceedingly full of undergrowth that often reached nearly to the tops of the rather scrubby trees. But as darkness descended and I made camp for the night, those scrubby trees seemed to grow into looming, staring things, and the undergrowth became alive, the breeze running through it like breath. I hadn't felt such a creeping up and down my backbone since I was a kid listening to my uncles tell ghost tales on the porch on summer nights.

Surely Minnie and Joben hadn't come this way. It aggravated me that not only had my misdirection left me out here in this spookish wilderness, but also had slowed me in catching up with them.

"Farleytown! Farleytown!" the parrot screeched out.

"Farleytown, eh?" I grumbled. "I hope that's where we'll find them—else I'll just see how good a parrot will roast on a spit."

Squatter came up, tongue lolling out and dripping, and looked to me for attention. I scratched behind his left ear. "Squatter, I'm glad you're here," I said. "I hate to admit to fearfulness, but I don't like this place. Not a bit."

I had bacon and flour, so I fried some of the former and made biscuits and a big shapeless loaf for Squatter from the latter. The parrot got crumbs, and Squatter ate his loaf smeared with bacon drippings. My beverage was boiled coffee, which I sipped on for an hour or so after the meal. I felt better then, not as wary as before. Soon my head was lolling and my brain growing fuzzy with the coming of sleep.

I jerked upright when Squatter came to his feet, bristling and growling. The parrot let out another "Farleytown!" The fire had died substantially, though enough flames licked up to cast a fair light a few feet around.

Grabbing up my rifle, I looked into the encircling forest. "Who's there? Who's there?"

The parrot echoed, "Who's there?"

"Shut up," I mumbled. Squatter, meanwhile, was

continuing his tense growling and edging forward inches at a time.

I kicked a few more sticks onto the fire and let them catch and brighten the scene. Something moved in the brush, and now Squatter sent up a loud, howling bark and looked at me. One command and he would launch into the woods to take on whatever, or whoever, was out there.

"Call off that hound," a rumbling voice said abruptly. It startled me to realize how close the unseen speaker was.

"Show yourself, or I'll turn him onto you," I replied.

The brush moved; Squatter growled like an empty belly as into the firelight stepped one of the strangest men I had ever seen. Back in boyhood I had once read of legends from across the ocean about spirits that inhabit the forest and are somehow an incarnation of trees and brush, leaves and wood. Those old stories were the first things through my mind as I examined the peculiar being before me.

His trousers were rags of wool held up by a rope. A hatchet was stuck into his belt on the left side, and a knife and rusty pistol on the right. His shirt was homemade and shapeless, looking like a particularly crude hunting shirt of the sort worn a century ago. My impression, however, was that this garb had not been made in imitation of any particular design. It was as if the man had simply thrown together a rough garment with a minimum of effort. His hat was of felt, very old and battered, and the front of the brim curled up toward the crown. The dirt-crusted face was bearded, and seemed pallid, though the rich firelight made that hard to be sure of.

And here was the feature that intrigued and then frightened me: The man wore brand new boots, store-bought boots, and obviously too big for him. How would such a poor old forest elf as this come by such a fine pair of boots? He wouldn't have the money to buy them, and even if he had, he surely would have bought boots to fit. It was obvious to me that these boots had come from someone else—probably a lost traveler, just like me. And I was willing to bet whoever gave up those boots hadn't done so willingly.

"Who are you, and why are you coming to a man's camp by night?" I asked with deliberate gruffness. I figured it best to grab the advantage here from the outset.

"I smelt your bacon, seen your light," the man said. "My name's Copper. Eb Copper."

"Well, if I'm trespassing on your land or something, I'm sorry. I didn't plan on it. I lost my way." I winced at my own ill-advised words. I had just informed this stranger that I was lost.

"Farleytown!" the bird said.

Abruptly, a second figure appeared, materializing out of the forest. He was younger than the first man, but no more kempt and clean, and no less ragged. His mouth lolled open as he stared at me, then he turned his gaze toward the parrot. The young fellow had no visible teeth. His hat was new; probably it had belonged to the same unfortunate whose boots now graced the older man's feet.

"Look-air, Papaw! Look-air 'at tawkin' bird!"

"This here's Iradell, my boy," Cooper said. "He likes your bird yonder."

"What do you want from me?"

"Cup of coffee. Biscuit, if you got it. We're lost too."

I didn't buy that. These men were too much part and parcel of this forest for me to believe this was an alien place to them.

"'At-air bird tawks! Tawks like a man!"

Lord knows I didn't want these men sharing my camp. Squatter's feelings apparently were similar; he was still in a stance for attack. But what could I do? If they intended ill for me, it was better to keep them within view than to send them out of sight.

"Help yourself to the coffee. I'm afraid the biscuits are gone—but I'll make more."

"You're right kind, and we thank you, Mister . . ."

"Cleveland. Hal Cleveland." I felt so mistrustful I didn't see cause even to give my own name, though it would have meant no more to them than the false one I presented.

"Cleveland . . . like the president."

"That's right. Uncle Grover and me, we're close. I suppose he'd send out the army to find me if ever I went missing."

Squatter dropped to his haunches and rested his big head on his paws, keeping an eye on Eb Copper. The younger woodsman, meanwhile, was at the parrot's cage, poking a finger through and guffawing every time the bird said a word.

I made biscuits with one eye on my work and the other on my unwanted guests. The passing of time did nothing to make me feel better about them.

"Where you heading?" Eb Copper asked.

"Just traveling farther south," I replied, not wanting to share any more information about myself than was essential. I was wondering how I was going to

manage to sleep with these two in my camp. Hang it,
I *wouldn't* sleep. How could I, feeling sure they would
bash my head in or shoot me as soon as I did?

"How 'at bird learn to tawk?"

"My wife taught it. It's her bird."

Ed Copper glanced around. "Wife? Where she
be?"

"On her way here with her brother. He's a federal
marshal," I said. "Though he nearly lost his job here a
while back for shooting a man without cause. He
didn't like the looks of the fellow, so he just pulled out
a shotgun and blasted him right in the loins. It was
ugly."

Copper's eye narrowed. He gnawed his biscuit
like a rat. He didn't seem much worried by the stories
I was telling. The thing that had him concerned was
closer at hand, tangible, and drooling.

"That dog there, how mean is he?"

"Not much mean, unless a man moves too quick
around him. Then he'll go for the neck, and I swear you
can't stop him once he does. He chewed the head off a
fellow one time. The poor old fool had made a move as
if to hurt me, and Squatter just went out-of-his-mind-
loco." I was doing my best lying in hopes of convincing
the two Coppers that it wasn't worth staying around to
pluck the feathers from this particular guinea.

Copper stood, stretched, and yawned, Squatter's
eye on him the entire time. "Mr. Cleveland, I'm weary.
Do you care if we share your camp tonight?"

Glumly I replied, "Make yourself comfortable."
There was nothing else I could say.

"Thank you, sir. I'll be proud to brag that I shared
a camp with the president's nephew."

"Wanna buy that bird," Iradell Copper said.

"Can't sell it. It's my wife's."

"Want that bird."

"Sorry."

The senior Copper was in the process of removing the hatchet from his belt. He reached for the pistol then, and I watched him intently. If anything was to happen, this seemed a likely moment.

"That's a fine dog you got, Mr. Cleveland. Yes indeedy. I reckon it would protect its master until its last breath, just as you've said."

"Reckon it would."

"That's why I have no choice but to do this, Mr. Cleveland." He pulled the pistol and shot Squatter, right there before my eyes.

"No!" I yelled. *"No!"*

Already Copper had picked up his hatchet and was advancing toward me, his expression very businesslike, for this indeed was nothing to him but business. It was if I were frozen in place, unable to move. His shooting of Squatter had stunned me into paralysis.

I broke out of it too late to dodge the blow. The hatchet went back, came forward, and pain, far more explosive and racking than that inflicted earlier by Manchester the wagoner, cracked like lightning in my head as the flat side of the hatchet struck me. I fell to my knees, then forward onto my face, landing partly atop Squatter.

He whimpered and moved beneath me. "Squatter . . ." I reached up to touch his twitching snout. Then Eb Copper appeared above me, squatting down to examine me.

"I reckon I didn't hit you hard enough," he said.

He hefted up the hatchet again. I closed my eyes and awaited the death blow.

5

I never knew why Eb Copper didn't kill me. Maybe I passed out at just the right moment and he thought I was already dead. Maybe some grain of mercy remained in his hardened old soul. All I know is that when I had opened my eyes and looked around, I was still in this world.

They had taken everything: guns, food, supplies, even the parrot. All that was left was me, dizzy, hurting, injured, staggering through the darkness on foot, carrying the bloody form of Squatter in my arms. It was cold and hellish. A drizzle fell, the same one that had chilled me back to consciousness. I didn't know where I was going; all I knew was I had to go. Had to keep moving.

Squatter was heavy, straining my muscles and making my twice-injured head ache all the more. Sometimes I would stop and put him down, crouching beside him and stroking him until my breath returned. Then I would pick him up again and proceed through the dark Ozark forest.

I caught myself thinking that it would have been better had they gone ahead and killed me. There remained enough of my old, rational self to repudiate that despairing notion. "It's good we are alive, Squatter," I said aloud. "As long as we're alive, we can keep going."

Squatter's blood encrusted my hands. Eb Copper's bullet had struck the dog in the hindquarters, shattering one of the back legs and leaving an ugly hole. At the beginning Squatter had howled and thrashed when I tried to pick him up. Gradually shock had numbed him, and now he whimpered like a pup as I struggled along. I was sure he would die. The thought made me cold inside.

At last I could go no farther. A hill rose beside me, with a round depression notched into its side. There dog and man collapsed and lay in a common heap, falling into a sleep that was more a stupor than a state of rest.

Morning light awakened me. I was stiff, cold, and aching. Moving, I heard a guttural canine groan. Squatter was still beside me, and still living. When I spoke to him, he wagged his tail weakly.

It crossed my mind that the merciful thing to do would be to strike him from behind with a big stone and end his suffering quickly. The thought never became action. This was Squatter, my most faithful companion. I couldn't bring myself to deliberately end his life.

Rising, I picked him up and began walking. Weakness overcame me; I discovered that the dime-novel depictions of people quickly shaking off head injuries like the kind I had suffered weren't very true to life. Never had I felt so dizzy and sick. Returning to the place we had spent the night, I lay down with the hound and raked leaves over us. We slept again.

The day dragged past, and we remained where

we were. A rain came, but we weren't much dampened, being sheltered by the hill, which was between us and the wind. A rivulet of water ran down a rocky portion of the hillside. Catching some of it in my hands, I drank, and gave some to Squatter as well.

Squatter's wound looked uglier and appeared to be beginning to fester. If that happened, I would have no choice but to find some way to mercifully end his life. I wouldn't let him die the terrible death of infection. If only I had a gun.

Night fell, and I was hungry. Squatter lived even yet . . . and maybe was a bit stronger. I hardly dared believe it, for fear of being disappointed.

I slept hard until morning, and when the light came, I was hungrier than ever, but feeling more stable, more my old self. When I stood, I wasn't as dizzy as I had been. And Squatter still hadn't died.

"Come on, boy," I said. "Today we're finding food. And if we can, help for you. We'll clean that wound, get you well again."

I started to examine the wound, then averted my eyes. The smell of it had struck my nose, and I knew what I would find if I looked. So I didn't look. I just picked up my old friend and started walking though the leafy Ozark hills.

The house seemed to be abandoned. I studied it closely from the cover of the trees for a long time before I dared step into the scrub-filled clearing in which it stood. Built unevenly of logs and roofed in the old style with boards instead of shingles, this must have been the refuge of some Ozark hermit.

Or perhaps of two—a father and son I was not eager to meet again, at least not under these circumstances. At some later time, when I was strong and evenly matched, I might welcome the chance to give my version of the time of day to Eb Copper and son.

The longer I examined the cabin, however, the less I suspected it was occupied by Copper or anyone else. The front door, though intact, stood open, and trash aplenty had been blown in through it. There was a big cobweb across one of the windows, which was broken out.

Rising, I carried Squatter to the door and looked in. Furniture of the roughest sort was inside, draped in cobwebs and covered with leaves and assorted grit that had blown in through the door and broken window. There was a stove in one corner, beside a closed cupboard. A ladder extended up to a loft above the single lower-level room.

"Hello?" I called out, weakly. No answer came.

Confident now that the place was indeed unoccupied, I carried my dog inside and lay him down on a pile of rags that apparently had been another dog's bed at some past time. Squatter was very weak now, and I was sure his last would come soon.

"If we're lucky, there'll be food somewhere here," I said. "But we can't bet on it, Squatter. Nobody would go off and just leave food."

I went to the cupboard and opened it, figuring I would find it empty. Instead, I looked in upon several cans of various foods, from peaches to beans. "What the devil's this?" I muttered. Why would anyone have simply abandoned their cabin without taking their food along?

Unless . . .

I glanced up at the loft, moved over to the ladder, put my hand and foot on it . . . then removed them.

"We'll eat first, Squatter," I said. "I'll look up yonder afterward."

There were knives, forks, and spoons in a pile beside the cans. With a knife, I pried open a can of pork meat and dumped it in front of Squatter. He lifted his head just enough to lick at the meat and drag it into his mouth with his tongue. There was very little strength left in the faithful old fellow, and sad it was to see.

I ate beans, peaches, and corn, and never had a meal gone down so well. The food tasted old, but I barely noticed. My stomach, too long empty, grumbled and growled as it adjusted to an overdue filling. I could feel my strength returning even before I downed the last bite.

Squatter was asleep by then, so I covered him with a tattered old blanket I had found. Slipping up into the loft, I set my nerve for what I expected to discover, and was surprised when it wasn't there. Descending, I glanced out a back window. A privy stood at a cockeyed angle across the backyard. There was no back door, so I had to circle around from the front to reach it.

Sure enough, he was in there, what remained of him after several months of death. He was collapsed on the floor of the privy, just a jumble of dried flesh and bone and hide and decaying clothing. I closed the door, swallowed, and hoped I wouldn't lose the meal I had just devoured.

That explained well enough why everything here seemed intact. The corpse had appeared to be that of an old man; I suppose he had been a hermit, just as I had initially thought. Likely I was the first living soul to set foot on this place in all the months since he had died.

I explored his cabin and found little worth the having, with one exception. A long twelve-gauge shotgun was leaned behind the cupboard, almost out of sight, along with a box and a half of shells. On the butt of the shotgun were the roughly carved initials H.J. I cleaned the weapon as best I could and loaded it. Hefting it, I smiled. Being armed again made me feel not so helpless. Let the Coppers come around now, and see how I greeted them!

"Thanks, H.J.," I said aloud. "I'll treat this weapon with care."

And then I thought of Squatter, and the satisfaction of again having a weapon vanished. Now I did have means to end his suffering . . . but did I want to?

I walked over to him, shotgun in hand. Trembling, I raised it, leveled the double barrels at his head . . . and he awakened and looked up at me.

The shotgun lowered; I couldn't do it.

"Squatter, poor old boy," I said, kneeling and putting my hand on his head. "Poor old loyal boy . . . God forgive me, but I just can't bring myself to end your life. I just can't do it."

Darkness found me sitting beside Squatter, knowing what my duty was but finding me still unable, or unwilling, to do it. At length my chin dropped and I dozed.

A noise, a movement outside the cabin . . .

I lifted my head too quickly, making the bruised places on my skull burst with pain. For several moments I had no idea where I was. There was something cold in my hand. I looked and saw the shotgun, and then I remembered.

Looking down to see how Squatter was, I was amazed to find his resting place vacant.

"Squatter?"

His familiar growl rumbled. In the darkness I could scarcely make him out, standing beside the door.

More movement outside, and not the movement of wind in the branches. The unmistakable movement of a man, or men.

If the Coppers were there, by heaven, I would make them wish they hadn't come around. I stood, fought dizziness a few moments, and advanced.

My caution was tempered with happiness at seeing Squatter on his feet again. Maybe he had turned a corner and would be well.·

He growled again, and sent out a little bark. He took a step forward, and the back of him collapsed, the wounded leg unable to sustain his weight. I knew then it was sheer force of will that had made him able to rouse from his rag bed. He had detected the creeping man outside and had risen to protect his master.

"Here, boy, nice dog . . ."

The voice came from outside. The man, whoever he was, had heard Squatter's growl. I was pleasantly surprised to realize the voice was different than that of either of the Coppers. Of course, that didn't mean this fellow was necessarily any less dangerous.

There was hardly any light, just a vague, imprecise moonlight that spilled in through the window. Footsteps outside . . . I was about to call out for the prowling man to identify and show himself, when suddenly there was a minuscule change in the shadows, and there he was, looking in the window.

I never knew where Squatter found the strength to make his leap, given that one of his hind legs was useless and he was weakened through and through. With a howl he shot from floor to window; the man outside yelled in fright. Man and beast vanished from my view.

"Squatter!" I shouted. "Squatter!"

Outside there was snarling and barking, cussing and yelling. I yanked open the door and went out. Lifting the shotgun, I fired the contents of one barrel into the sky. The flash and roar of the twelve-gauge was impressively authoritative. The man, whoever he was, cussed again and loped into the woods. Squatter went after him, but he faltered and collapsed.

I ran to him. He rolled onto his side, looking up at me, whimpering. His exertion had taken the last of his strength.

"Good boy, good dog—looking out for me to the end, huh? Good dog."

There wasn't enough light to let me see his eyes clearly, but I could feel the plea in them. I knew what I had to do. Bending down, I nuzzled my face against his ear.

"Good-bye, Squatter. Good-bye. I love you, boy."

The rest I did quickly, so as not to lose the necessary will. Standing, I aimed, closed my eyes, squeezed the trigger.

The roar was the most jolting thing I had ever heard. It rang in my ears, then faded into a silence that seemed to ring even louder. An empty, hollow ringing that wouldn't end.

I knelt beside him and reached down to stroke his fur. But I wouldn't look at him, not just yet. I wanted to touch him while he was yet warm, and think of him for a few more minutes as being as he had always been.

Inside I had the most aching feeling. But I knew I had done the right thing. He would suffer no more.

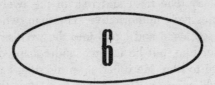

6

I continued through the forest a day later, feeling more alone than I had ever been. I had remained at the little cabin long enough to get more of my strength back, and to lay Squatter to rest. Once his grave was filled, I decided to dig a second and bury the bones of the old hermit whose remote home had given me refuge. It seemed the decent thing to do; no man should have to go back to the dust from which he came while lying on the floor of a privy.

As I traveled, I kept my eyes open for the sign of any human presence. I was thinking not only of the Coppers, but also of the lone man who had appeared at the cabin window. There had been no sign of him since Squatter ran him off, but one never knew, and the man might be angry over the way he had been treated. If so, he might not treat me very kindly should he come across me alone in the woods. I was glad I had the shotgun.

The remnants of a footpath led from the cabin and through the forest. Figuring this must have been the old hermit's pathway to civilization, I stuck with it.

The terrain here was remarkably uneven and convoluted, and at times I felt as if I was crossing my own path. It reminded me of my father's old joke about walking a mountain trail in Kentucky that was so twisted that he met himself coming around a bend.

It wasn't in my destiny to meet myself in such a manner today, but I was to run across a familiar old companion, and some acquaintances I would have preferred not to meet. It all happened very unexpectedly.

Walking through a rugged, area of limestone bluffs and springs that gushed up from the ground, I stopped abruptly when I heard a voice, shrilly cussing. The voice I knew very well; the words it was speaking, however, were quite out of character, for we had always been careful never to let the parrot pick up foul language.

I melted back into the trees and began looking around for the bird. Something fluttered in a treetop nearby, and I spotted it there. It was Minnie's parrot, all right, and he was cussing like a sailor. Obviously Iradell Copper had been busy teaching his kind of vocabulary to his ill-gotten pet. I wondered how the parrot had manage to get away from him.

"Bird! Hey, bird! Whur-ye be, bird?"

The proximity of the speaker startled me. I ducked deeper into my cover and began looking about for Iradell. At the same time, I drew the shotgun closer. If need be, I'd use it.

Iradell Copper came striding up the path, and I swear I smelled him before I saw him. He had an angry look on his face, and the empty cage in his hand.

"Come 'ere, bird, come 'ere afore I skin ya."

If Iradell was here, his father probably was as

well. Yet as I looked around, I detected no sign of him. Iradell hadn't seen me. Two options faced me: I could remain where I was and probably escape detection, or I could rise, level the shotgun on the mountaineer, and declare my intention to regain the goods he and his father had stolen from me.

The latter was tempting, especially when I considered that the Coppers were responsible for Squatter's wounding. Even so, it made more practical sense to lie still and let the situation pass. After all, if Eb Copper was nearby, it would be two men against one, and even though I had a shotgun, those odds weren't good.

Something moved farther down the path. It was a horse—*my* horse, stolen from me. Seeing that roused a seething anger inside. Then I noticed that Iradell was wearing my gun belt, and practicality gave way to fury. I'd be hanged before I'd let Iradell Copper go away from here on my horse, wearing my gun. For that matter, it was my parrot he was trying to recapture too, at least far more mine than his.

Noting that Eb Copper was still nowhere in sight, I gave into my impulse and stood, leveling the shotgun right at Iradell's midsection. He was so startled that he cussed, stepped back and tripped on a root. That left him on his rump, looking up at me with his mouth gaped open. Come to think of it, I hadn't seen him when his mouth *wasn't* gaped open.

"Hello, Iradell Copper," I said. "You remember me?"

"Don't shoot me, don'cha shoot me!"

"I won't—if you'll be so kind as to give me back what you took from me."

"Ain't never took nothin' from ya!"

"You really are stupid, ain't you? That gun you're wearing, that horse back yonder, even that parrot up in the tree—it's all mine, and you stole it from me, you and your mangy father."

"Ain't never seen ya! Ain't never stole nothin' from ya!"

I began to see how deficient this fellow really was. He truly thought there was something to be gained by denying a guilt as obvious as his. I would realize later that he had been trained to do that by his father, and lacked the sense to see when such a course was futile.

"Get up," I ordered.

He came to his feet. Nervous now, he was drooling at the lip, and didn't even bother to wipe it away.

"Take off that gun belt, very slow."

He did, and let it drop.

"Now back up, into the woods, and wrap your arms around that pine there."

He didn't budge.

"I said for you to back up and . . ."

Iradell was looking past me, and grinning now. I shifted to the side to keep him in view while also looking behind me.

"A man don't like seeing another man holding a shotgun on his own boy." Eb Copper said the words coldly. His expression was serious. Almost as serious as the rifle leveled on me. My rifle, the one he had stolen.

"You'd best drop that rifle, Copper," I said. "Else you'll see your boy cut in half when I empty these barrels."

"You wouldn't do that."

"I would indeed."

"No you wouldn't. Because you know that as soon as you pull that trigger, you'll be a dead man."

I swung the gun around and trained it on him. We stood facing off, shotgun against rifle.

"Maybe you're right," I said. "So now maybe I'll just cut you in half instead of your boy. That way, when I pull the trigger, it's you who'll be the dead man."

"I'll shootcha! I'll shootcha!"

Blast it all, I had just made a big blunder. Even as I had turned the gun on the senior Copper, the junior had reached down and pulled the Colt from my stolen gun belt. Now I was caught. I could kill one Copper, certainly, but would only be cut down myself by the survivor.

"Good bird! Cracker for the good bird!" the parrot squawked above my head.

The old man had the boy tie me to a tree, my back against the trunk and my hands roped together on the far side. It was a big tree, and Iradell did his best to make my hands meet, so that when he finished I felt as if I were stretched on one of those medieval racks. The father and son stepped back and looked at me like sculptors admiring a completed masterpiece.

"We going to leave 'im, Papaw?"

"No sirree, son. We're going to shoot him."

"You won't get away with this, Copper," I said. "This is murder, out and out murder. They'll put you on the gallows for it."

"No, they won't. They'd have to catch me, you see, and that's something ain't nobody been able to do. And what do I care if I got to murder a man? You ain't the first, friend. Me and Iradell, we make our way in this world by doing what we have to. Sometimes we have to take a life or two. That's just they way things go."

"Let me shoot 'im, Papaw! "Let me!"

"No, Iradell. Not yet. I want the first shot."

First shot ... that phrase implied that the first shot wouldn't be the last. Eb Copper intended to have his cruel fun before he completed this job. I pulled at my ropes, wishing I could get at him.

"Use 'at-air shotgun, Papaw! Shoot his leg bones!"

"That's a good idea, Iradell. I got to hand it to you for good ideas."

The old mountaineer laid down the rifle and picked up the shotgun. He opened it, checked the shells, and slammed it shut again. Meanwhile, I was praying what I was sure would be my final prayer, and wishing I had prayed a few more prayers back in the days when death wasn't staring me in the face.

"Well, friend, it's just too bad for you that you couldn't just leave things be. You had to come picking on my Iradell. I don't stand for such as that. Got no choice but to kill you."

"When they hang you, my ghost will be there to watch," I said. I was talking with bravado, but my mind was full of pictures—Minnie, my mother, my late father, and scenes of the life we had lived.

"Well, let's get it done," he said. He lifted the shotgun and squinted down the double barrel.

"Farleytown!" the parrot said.

I fought back the urge to close my eyes. In no way was I going to give Copper the satisfaction of seeing me cringe. It was all I could do to keep my eyes on him.

The roar came more quickly than I had expected, and made me yell. For a couple of seconds the world became unreal. Time had frozen. Then I began to realize things, one by one.

First off, the shotgun that had fired hadn't been the one in Eb Copper's hands. Second, Eb Copper no longer retained the shotgun. For that matter, he no longer retained the top of his head; someone had fired a blast of buckshot into his skull from a thicket of old briars about fifteen feet to the side. It made a messy and unpleasant sight. Third, Iradell Copper was scrambling for the shotgun his father had dropped when he fell dead. He got it, swung it around, and fired wildly into the thicket. I heard a grunt of pain, followed by another shotgun blast that sent fragments of briar bushes spitting out from the thicket. Iradell was struck in the chest, and died on the way to the ground.

I'm not too proud to confess that I fainted dead away right then from the shock of what I had just seen. If you think it was unmanly of me to do that, I ask you to think about what it would be like to be tied up and awaiting a torturous dispatching, only to have such a horror suddenly occur right in front of you. Then ask yourself if you think you would have done any better.

Awakening, I sat up. No longer was I tied to the tree; I was on the ground, well away from it. Glancing over, I saw the gory bodies of the two Coppers, and gave strong consideration to passing out again.

"Just don't look at them," a man's voice said. I turned and saw him, sitting on his haunches, his sawed-off shotgun laid across his lap and his hands tucked up under his overleaning upper body, out of sight. He was a thin, white-bearded man dressed in canvas pants, a thick cotton shirt, black wool coat, and slouch hat. He grinned, showing straight but yellow teeth. "That's the trouble with shotguns. They do so durn much damage. 'Specially these cut-down varieties."

I groaned and laid back down. "I thank you, sir, for saving my life."

"Glad to oblige. I take no pleasure in killing any living soul, but there's times it must be done. Them two, I reckon they earned it."

"My name's Enoch Brand. I'm from Fort Scott, Kansas."

"Well, sir, my name's Lee. Leviticus Lee. And I come from anyplace worth coming from, and several that ain't."

Rolling to the side, I pulled myself back upright, and then settled into a seated position amid the fallen autumn leaves. Looking at Lee, a strange feeling began to form itself somewhere in the pit of my stomach and churn upward through me. It was a kind of combination of joy, terror, relief, sorrow, and most every other feeling you could think of, and when it rose as high as my throat, it came out in uncontrollable laughter, the kind that isn't far from weeping. You've probably seen that happen before at particularly tragic funerals, or maybe even experienced it yourself.

Leviticus Lee seemed to enjoy my display. He grinned, then the laughter spread to him, and we sat guffawing together, while the two deceased Coppers lay in their death blood not twenty feet away. Looking back at it with the hindsight of so many years, it all seems pretty morbid.

"How'd you come across them two?" Lee asked.

I told him how they had come into my camp, eaten my food, knocked me cold, and shot my dog.

"So that dog was wounded when he come at me, huh? My, that must have been quite the critter!"

I was surprised. "That was you at the window? You that Squatter went after?"

"Indeed it was. Lord knows it surprised me too. All I was doing was looking for a roof for the night. Last time I was through here, there was a feller living there. Known as sort of a hermit, but he'd put folks up who needed it."

"When were you through last?"

"It's been many a year, young man. Many a long year, and a long mile."

I told him I had found the hermit's body in the privy, and buried it beside Squatter. Lee seemed to think that a generous thing to do.

"Mr. Brand, you're a fine young man. That I can see. I'm glad I run across you."

"Even though my dog took after you?"

"A good hound looks out for its keeper."

I stood and stretched my legs. It was awfully good to be alive when I fully expected to be dead by now. I expressed the sentiment to Lee.

"I'm glad you're feeling good . . . maybe you can help me out here a minute."

"Just name it."

So far he had sat with his hands tucked up and the shotgun under his torso as he leaned forward over his haunches. Now he lifted his left hand and held it up.

It was about enough to make me faint again. Almost half of Lee's hand was gone, just ripped away. I recalled the grunt of pain that had come from the thicket as Iradell Copper fired that last panicked shot into the brush. The pellets must have caught Lee right in the hand.

I went to him and helped him get seated against a tree, and went to work at once to clean and bandage the ugly wound as best the resources of the moment and place would allow. I was thinking, as I worked, of how this had been the bloodiest, most violent, most frightening day I had experienced in my life.

There was no way for me to know then that before my time with Leviticus Lee was past, there would be much more of the same to come my way, more trouble and adventure than I had ever figured to run across.

7

We recovered both my stolen horses, my guns, and—with effort—I even managed to catch the parrot and get it back into its cage. Leviticus Lee was riding an old mule; somehow that didn't surprise me. It seemed to fit.

My new companion was an odd fellow, but I liked him. How could I not like a man who had saved me from death at the hands of two mountain murderers? That event had forged an instant bond between me and Lee. And when I found he was bound for the Farleytown area, like I was, I determined to accompany him and find some way to repay the great favor he had done me.

Lee had little to say about himself, leaving me to figure out what I could about him on my own. He did explain his odd name when he mentioned having a late brother named Genesis and a sister named Exodus, who now resided with a husband in New York City. He hadn't seen her in twenty years.

I put Lee's age at about sixty, but I wasn't at all sure about it. He might have been younger by as much as a decade. I say this because everything about the man gave evidence of a difficult life, the kind that can put age on a man before his time. It was in his bearing, his way of talking, his attitude. Lee was a jovial man, yet hardened. Friendly, yet isolated.

He didn't ask me my business, but I told him anyway. In fact, I was just about bubbling over with the need to talk, simply to relieve the tension that had built up in me over my past days of suffering and trial. He found my dedication to finding my wayward wife interesting and maybe unreasonable, given what she had done. Yet he made no effort to change my thinking about her, as some might have. Lee was the type of man who left others to their own way of thinking, asking only that they give him the same freedom.

He knew the terrain, though not with the familiarity of one who had been upon it recently. He informed me that I had never been as lost as I had thought; Farleytown was within a day's ride. He figured he could get us there easily enough, unless the area had changed so much since the early sixties that he didn't recognize the old landmarks.

The early sixties ... that let me know that Lee hadn't been here since the war. Maybe he had been a soldier. I tucked that piece of supposition away, not thinking it particularly significant at the time.

I let Lee lead the way, and thought all was well, until I noted that our trail had led around to a place we had passed an hour before. We had traveled in a circle.

As I pointed this out to Lee, I suddenly noticed that sweat was pouring off his brow, even though the day was very cool. He held his injured hand tightly against himself; the bandage had soaked through with blood.

"Mr. Lee, I believe that hand is making you sick," I said. "Maybe we ought to put up for a while and let you rest."

"Maybe you're right, Mr. Brand."

Lee wouldn't let me examine his wound, saying it hurt too much to fiddle with it. After we had rested a couple of hours, I suggested that perhaps we should go on. Lee fidgeted and asked if I would mind reaching Farleytown tomorrow rather than today; he was feeling rather peaked and thought it might be well for him to travel no farther today.

I agreed, but with such obvious reluctance that he tried to send me on ahead alone. "There's no cause for you to be held back by a pokey old badger like me. You go on alone—just stick with that trail."

"That's the trail that brought us circling back to here," I replied. "I'd just get myself lost, going alone. Besides, if you're puny, you might need some tending. I don't mind staying."

Truthfully, I did mind a little. I had already had enough of camping in the Ozark woodlands. Besides, too much delay might result in Minnie and Joben going on out of Farleytown—if ever they had gone there at all—and me losing their track completely.

Yet there was nothing else to do but remain. Owing Leviticus Lee my life as I did, I could hardly run out on him while he was feeling sick.

Night came, and still he kept his injured hand to himself, swearing it needed no attention. Clearly it did. He passed the night in great pain, and by morning I was certain that the shattered hand was putrefying. Already some miscoloration was visible between his cuff and the base of the crude bandage.

"Mr. Lee, we've got to get you into Farleytown and to a doctor. I'm fearing you might be bound to lose that hand."

"I've lost many a hand in my day. But just in poker. Not like this." He laughed, but it really wasn't funny either to me or him.

"Come on, Mr. Lee," I said. "Let's get riding."

I had already readied the horses. Lee rose to head for his—and staggered. Sitting back down hard, right on the ground, he leaned to the side and became sick.

I knew then the hand really was turning bad, and with frightening speed. When he was through with his heaving, I helped him up and managed to get him into the saddle. It was anybody's guess right then whether he would be able to stay in it all the way to Farleytown—and anybody's guess whether we would even be able to find the place.

Fortune smiled, and by following a new fork in the trail, I led us to a wagon road. Heading southwest, it widened, until at last farms and houses came into view.

Farleytown itself was still a mile ahead when Leviticus Lee fell from his saddle. I stopped, ran to him, and knew as soon as I examined the hand that Lee was a sick man indeed.

What to do? He was half senseless, obviously in no shape to ride. To make a litter would take too much time. Looking around, I spotted a two-story house, just visible on the other side of a narrow strip of woodland. If it had been summer, with foliage full, the house would have been invisible.

"Mr. Lee, I'm going to try to get you to yonder house, and see if we can't get a wagon or something to carry you to the doctor. You understand me?"

From its perch on the back of one of the horses, the caged parrot repeated, "Mr. Lee! Mr. Lee!"

"Can you hear 'em coming?" Lee asked fearfully. He stiffened, looked around as if frightened. "The Yanks! I can hear 'em! Listen!"

He was out of his head already. I hadn't known it was so bad. If only he hadn't hid the mounting infection from me, perhaps we could have found some way to deal with the problem before now.

"There's no Yanks here, Mr. Lee. They've been gone more than twenty years now. Come on—let me get you up."

With great struggle I got him to his feet. The prospect of trying to get him onto a horse, even in the belly-down dangling position, was unthinkable. Despite his rather spare build, Leviticus Lee carried a good amount of weight. Or maybe I was just weaker than usual because of all that had happened the last few days.

The curving drive leading through the trees toward the house was really nothing more than a couple of wagon-wheel ruts cut through the woods floor. We had circled halfway around to the house when I heard the rumble of a vehicle approaching behind us. Lee's right arm was draped over my shoulder and I was carrying most of his weight, so it took me a couple of seconds to get us turned around to face the new arrival.

The approaching vehicle was a very creaky buckboard. The driver, an ample fellow dressed in a nice but wrinkled suit of clothes, and wearing a thin mustache on a wide face, pulled the buckboard to a stop, slid on some spectacles that had been in his coat pocket, and eyed us up and down.

"Are you the men who left those horses and such on the road back there?"

"Yes, sir. My name is Enoch Brand. This man with me is Leviticus Lee, and he's hurt. Is that your house ahead?"

"Indeed."

"Well, sir, then you're the man we're seeking. Mr. Lee has been injured in the hand, and the wound is going bad on us. I had wanted to get him to Farleytown, but he has become too sick to ride. If you have a wagon we could cart him on ..."

"I can do you better than that, Mister ... Brand, did you say? Take him on to the house, and I'll send my boy to fetch Dr. Ruscher from town."

"I thank you, sir. You're a truly charitable soul."

His name, he said, was Fairweather, Robert Elroy Fairweather, and he was a merchant in Farleytown. He ran a big general store—a store at a crossroads that I would ultimately find pretty much *was* Farleytown— and he provided space upstairs for a retired old physician out of Memphis who had settled in Farleytown to enjoy some ease in his old age. Despite his officially retired status, Dr. J. B. Ruscher was kind enough to keep hours a day or two a week and dispense medical care to the Farleytown people. Quite kind of him, didn't I think?

I agreed that surely it was kind, and in the current situation, might be of life-or-death importance. I didn't worry about saying such a thing with Lee right there to hear it, for clearly he was in a world of his own right now, raving and talking about Yanks and gunshots . . .

And gold coins. Something imprecise and vague and garbled, but those two words made their way out of the welter of nonsense and into my ear. And I could tell that Fairweather heard them too, could tell it from the way his face looked pinched and sharp for just a second . . . could tell it from the way he and I both fell silent for another second thereafter.

The Fairweather family, a sizable bunch, met us on the porch of the house, and Fairweather barked instructions to what looked to be his oldest son. The boy nodded, ran back to the buckboard, turned it, and drove it toward town. And when we had gotten Lee inside and onto a bed in the nearest bedroom, Fairweather sent two more boys out to bring in the horses Lee and I had been forced to abandon on the road.

I sank into a chair, took a deep breath, and closed my eyes in battle against a mounting headache that had started at the base of my skull and was advancing forward. Meanwhile, the Fairweather children—how many were there, anyway? A dozen?—stirred and talked excitedly among themselves, as youngsters will do, and made sounds of disgust when Fairweather pulled away Lee's clotted bandage to reveal the mangled thing that had been a hand.

Fairweather looked at me sternly. "Mr. Brand, it looks to me as if this wound was the result of a shotgun blast."

"It was," I said.

"How did it happen?"

I thought about the terrible incident in the forest,

and of Eb and Iradell Copper falling dead from the blasts of Leviticus Lee's sawed-off. How should I answer Fairweather? I wanted to tell the truth—but might the truth result in charges coming against Lee, the very man who had saved my life? I knew nothing of the law; such a thing seemed very possible to me.

And so I lied. "It was my fault," I said. "I dropped a shotgun and it went off. Thank God it hit his hand and not his head."

"Yes. Yes." Fairweather looked at the hand again. "I do hope Dr. Ruscher will hurry."

I stood there, feeling bad for having lied, and wondering if ill would come of it. My mother had always told me that falsehoods carry the price of trouble. I hoped she was wrong.

Leviticus Lee jerked and yelled and said something else about gold—and once again Fairweather and I both pretended we hadn't heard it, while both knew that we had, and that the words had sparked the start of something fierce and greedy in us.

It's a cursed substance, gold. It has brought more tragedy to mankind than anything except maybe the thirst for power. The lust for gold is a destroying lust. I know that now, as an elderly man writing a narrative of an old but clear memory. I learned that bit of wisdom, you see, back in Arkansas in 1886. Learned it so bitterly that I never have been able to forget it.

But at the time I stood in Fairweather's house, beside Leviticus Lee's bed, waiting for the arrival of Dr. J. B. Ruscher, the learning and the bitterness still lay ahead, for me, Leviticus Lee, and the Fairweather family alike.

8

The Fairweather boy who went to town for the doctor must have made a big show of his mission, for when he returned with the aging sawbones, he was followed by a half-dozen local stragglers who wanted to know who the excitement was all about.

"There's a man here, a stranger, named Leviticus Lee, and he's been injured," Robert Fairweather announced to them from his porch. "With him is this gentleman, Mr. Enoch Brand. Now, if you folks will be going, perhaps we can return some semblance of order to this place."

"Leviticus Lee? What loco kind of name is that?" one of them asked.

"An odd one, that's all," Fairweather replied. "Now, be off with you."

Dr. Ruscher, though very old, seemed to know his business. He examined Lee's hand, inquired how it had been hurt (prompting me to repeat my lie—with a little less feeling of guilt this time, the conscience being the most malleable and easily worn-down of man's capacities), and announced that in all likelihood the hand would have to be amputated.

"But there may yet be hope," he said. "I want to stay here through the night, Robert, and see if there is any sign of improvement. If not, I'll have to take it off in the morning."

We moved Lee to an upstairs bedroom, banishing two of the Fairweather sons to sleep in the barn loft. Dr. Ruscher, as good as his word, settled into a chair to pass the night beside Leviticus Lee. I already appreciated the old physician's dedication. How many retired doctors would have gone to this much trouble for a stranger?

I put the parrot's cage into Lee's sickroom to keep Dr. Ruscher company. "It talks, and I'm afraid it's taken up cussing," I said. "It wasn't me or Mr. Lee who taught it that. Just some troublemakers we ran across."

"I'm sure it won't say anything I haven't heard aplenty before now," the doctor said.

When I left the room, he was trying to prompt the bird to talk. Leviticus Lee, meanwhile, was tossing and jabbering out of his head, as before, and I caught myself listening for another mention of gold coins.

Now that things had settled down somewhat, I was able to properly thank the Fairweather family for their hospitality. I counted a total of seven children, five of them boys, and all resembling their father more than their mother.

Speaking of the mother, it was clear from her looks that she didn't much like having two strangers present in her house, and I couldn't much blame her. Lee had already bled on the rug and two beds. But I didn't think that was the real source of her sour attitude.

Blanche Fairweather had already picked up on the fact that Lee had been injured by a shotgun blast. It was my clear impression that she wasn't confident that my tale about an accident was true. Maybe it was some sort of intuition she possessed; whatever, the looks she gave me were the sort you would give a stranger you suspected of having stolen your best china. I tried to be friendly and look harmless, but this didn't make any difference in her ways around me.

"Mr. Brand, how long do you think you'll be staying with us?" she asked me as she busied about to make supper.

"Blanche!" her husband cut in. "What a rude question! Mr. Brand and Mr. Lee are welcome here as long as need be." He looked at me and smiled, one of those too-big smiles like the deacons give visitors at the front door of the church on Sunday mornings. "Besides, my dear, I think these men will prove to be good friends to this family."

Now, what did he mean by that? I figured he had in mind those gold coins Leviticus Lee had raved about, and hoped to get his hands on a few. What he couldn't know, of course, was that I was in no position to help him on that score. I had no idea what or where those coins were supposed to be. They might have been the figment of a raving man's fevered imagination, as far as I knew.

I secretly resented the interest that I sensed Fairweather held in the gold. Lee was *my* partner, not his. If anyone shared in any gold, it should be me.

Without my realizing it, Leviticus Lee had made a jump in my mind from traveling companion to partner. Was it only because of my gratitude to him for saving my life . . . or was I also succumbing to the lure of the mysterious treasure he raved about?

Lee was worse, not better, in the morning, and Dr. Ruscher announced that an amputation was required. "I want you to help me, Mr. Brand."

"Me? Listen, doctor, I'm not too good with blood and such. I might just be in your way . . . especially if I passed out on you."

"I need your help. Blood is blood, and we've all got it, so you can just get over sweating about it. If you're weak of stomach, by gum, you need to be broken of that foolish weakness anyway. I got no patience for the weak of stomach. By gum, where would the world be if we men of medicine turned weak of stomach? Answer me that one!"

Blanche Fairweather scowled at me from the hallway as I entered the room with Dr. Ruscher to begin the operation. Even after I closed the door, I fancied I could feel her angry gaze boring through it.

The doctor had already wrapped Lee's wrist in a cloth soaked in some sort of acidic liquid, maybe carbolic acid, to kill the germs on his skin. With a strong-smelling liquid soaked into a cloth, he put Lee to sleep, and informed me that part of my task would be to make sure he remained knocked out throughout the surgery. He then began cleaning Lee's putrefied wound with a solution that he said was forty grains of chloride of zinc to the ounce of water. "It cleans away the source of the putridity," he explained.

I was already beginning to turn green, and when he got down to the actual business I had to squeeze my eyes shut out of fear I would faint dead away. The doctor didn't let me get away with that for long, however, because I was of no use to him blind.

"Open your eyes and help me keep this arm elevated," he ordered. "You need to man the tourniquet. Come on, man, get hold of yourself! I've got no time for squeamishness. I have to wonder how far medicine would advance if not for folks going all white and pukish every time they see a little blood."

"Sorry," I muttered, and determined to hold my own no matter what.

It was one of the hardest things I have ever done, or ever will do. Dr. Ruscher was a good physician, but even the best amputation job results in more squirting blood and gruesome noises of flesh-and-bone-slicing than anyone would ever want to see or hear. Three or four times I was sure I would faint right there, but with great effort I managed to hold up. When it was all over and Leviticus Lee's stump was neatly bandaged, I sent up a fervent prayer of thanks for an ordeal ended.

"I'm no judge of doctoring, but it appears to me you did that well," I said rather shakily.

"I've removed many a limb, son, back during the war. It's a bad thing to have to do to any man, but better to lose limb than life."

"What will you do with the hand?"

"I'm giving it to you."

"What?" I blanched and waved him off. "No thank you. I got no use for it."

"I'm not joshing with you. Mr. Lee was lucid enough during one stretch last night for me to explain that I was going to have to remove his hand. He agreed, and told me to give it to you for a burial. He said it had been a fine appendage to him, and he

wanted it treated properly, not just burned up as rubbish."

"You're really not joshing with me, Doc?"

"I'm not."

"Lord have mercy."

About dusk I set out to fulfill Leviticus Lee's unusual request. The hand, wrapped up in several layers
of butcher paper, was in a wooden box I had begged
off Fairweather. The box was bigger than necessary,
and I had stuffed sawdust and shavings around the
enwrapped hand, and tacked down the box top.

I told no one what I was doing, and rode alone.
Out the road a ways, I turned right and entered the
woods, riding until the undergrowth was too thick for
the horse. I left the horse there and walked on across
a rise, carrying the box, shovel, and my rifle, which I
had brought along in case I ran across any trouble-
some woodland critters.

One thing about digging a grave for a hand instead of an entire body: It doesn't take long. And that
was good, for it was growing dark on me and I didn't
want to have to make my way back to the road without
light.

I cast the shovel aside, put the box in the hole,
and prepared to fill in the hole again. Then I stopped.
It didn't seem right to bury part of a man without at
least some words being said. But what did you say
when you were funeralizing a hand?

"Lord," I said, with hands folded before me and
head lowered, "I've come here this evening to lay to
rest the left hand of Leviticus Lee. I'm sure it's been
a good hand to him. Thank you for giving him use of
it for the years he had it, and I hope you'll let him

keep its partner for the rest of his days. And that the stump won't hurt him too much while it heals. Amen."

Then I filled the hole, tamped down the dirt, and rolled a couple of nearby rocks in place above the mound. It was getting very dark now; it appeared I'd be going home without the light after all. I hoped I'd have no trouble finding where I had left the horse.

A stirring in the brush behind me . . .

I wheeled. "Who's there?"

No one answered. Might it have been an animal? Just in case, I picked up my rifle, took a step toward the place the noise had come from . . .

Someone moved—not something, but someone, for I could tell it was human—and made a wild scrambling. I raised the rifle.

"I hear you in there! State your business, and show yourself! Why have you been watching me?"

More scrambling; I wondered if whoever it was had caught his foot on a root or in a tangle.

"All right, I'm coming to face you, and you'd best—"

I cut off with a yell when a gunshot sounded in the thicket and a slug sped past my head. Shards of blasted leaves rocked slowly to earth at the thicket's edge. Now it was my turn to scramble. Ducking to the side, I rolled behind a stump, lifted the rifle and re-flexively returned fire. A man's voice sent up a yell and cuss, and then I heard him tear free out of the thicket and run off through the dark woods.

Slowly I stood. When I was satisfied that he was gone, I advanced. There was no light now, and no way to examine the thicket for evidence of who it might have been.

I was mystified, and scared. Whoever it was, he

had shot at me in a way that indicated he meant business. But why? I knew no one here, and had made no enemies in Arkansas but the Coppers, and they were dead.

The horse was still there, and I led it out to the road and mounted. By now I was worried. What if the man I had shot died and they blamed me? How could I prove he had fired the first shot? What if they looked back at my trouble in Kansas, tied it together with this, and decided I was such a troublemaker that I needed to be put away for many years? As I've penned here previously, I knew nothing of the law and what could and couldn't be done. Anything, no matter how dreadful, seemed possible to me.

That night I said nothing of what had happened, not even to Lee. Of course, he was sleeping under the influence of laudanum and was therefore no partner for conversation anyway. The doctor had gone home, promising to return the next day.

"Where have you been?" Blanche Fairweather demanded when I showed up. The bluntness of the question took me back a little, but I supposed she was so used to keeping tabs on her own boys that she had gotten into the habit of forthrightness.

"I had an errand," I said.

"Supper was an hour ago. I fixed a good meal, and you didn't even have the common decency to come to the table."

"I'm sorry. I didn't mean to anger you, Mrs. Fairweather."

"I had to feed that friend of yours upstairs with my own hands, and I didn't much like that either. I was expecting you to do that. It seems the least you could do to repay our kindness to you. I don't have time to be nursemaid to a stranger with a household this size to tend to."

Robert Fairweather walked into the room, and looked aghast when he caught on to the way she was harping at me. This lady made my Minnie, no poor hand at the harping business herself, seem downright kind by contrast. "Dear wife, don't be so harsh with our guest!" Fairweather looked at me, smiling that oversized smile. "Mr. Brand, was that my shovel I saw you carrying back into the barn?"

"Yes, sir. I hope you didn't mind me borrowing it."

"Not at all. You had something to dig up, perhaps?"

"No. To bury."

"Ahhh!" The sparkle in his eye let me know just what he was thinking, and I despised him for it, despite his friendliness. I could read him so easily; he figured me and Leviticus Lee as potential sources of gain, and that was the reason for this exaggerated joviality and kindness of his. Maybe the initial kindness had been true charity, but now . . .

"It was Mr. Lee's hand," I said.

His face fell. "Oh. I see."

I turned to Mrs. Fairweather. "Ma'am, I can tell I anger you, and I'm sorry about it. It wasn't my plan to impose upon you, and I pledge to you we'll be out of your hair as soon as possible. I came to Arkansas to find a straying wife, and there's no need for me to stay here to look for her. If you want, I'll move on out, and come back and get Mr. Lee as soon as he's fit to travel."

She looked hopeful, then peered at her husband, who stepped up and said, "Nonsense, nonsense, Mr.

Brand. I insist you remain with us as long as you are in the area. And Mr. Lee as well, of course."

I glanced at Mrs. Fairweather to see how she would react. "He's the man of the house," was all she said, turning quickly on her heel and walking back into the kitchen.

"Blanche has a harsh side to her—don't mind it," Fairweather said. "I'll have a word about it with her later."

"No, sir, please don't, not on my account." I could just imagine how she would despise me after being chewed over by her husband about her treatment of me.

"No, no, I don't mind it a bit," he said. "Come in, Mr. Brand, have a cigar with me, if you would. Let me get to know you better."

"Well, thank you, sir, but I'd best be seeing how Mr. Lee is doing upstairs."

"He's fine, fine—just checked on him myself. He's sleeping, so we won't bother him."

I was still shaky from the mysterious shooting encounter in the forest, and hoped my hands weren't trembling too much when I lit the cigar. Meanwhile, Blanche Fairweather walked in, bearing a tray with my supper on it. She set it down before me, on the foot table in front of the sofa.

"I don't let the boys eat in here, but you can, Mr. Brand. You get special treatment here, you see." Her sarcasm had quite an edge.

When she was gone, I wished I could get up and run out. The Fairweather house was becoming an unpleasant place to be. I just wanted to find Minnie, take her back from Joben Malan (if I could figure out how to do it), and get on toward Tennessee.

Of course, if I did that, then I wouldn't know what Leviticus Lee had been talking about when he mentioned the gold coins. And the truth was, I was just as hungry as Robert Fairweather was to know about that.

He leaned back and blew smoke upward. "Buried a hand! What a task! Heh, heh, heh!" His laugh seemed as false as his comradery. "So that was all it was, huh? Just Mr. Lee's hand?"

"What else would it have been?"

"Eh? Oh, I don't know. Just talking, that's all. Moving my jaws to hear the hinges squeak, you know. Heh, heh!"

It was a long evening before I broke free of him and got to my pallet bed. Even after I did, I couldn't sleep, because I was thinking about the shooting incident in the forest, because Blanche Fairweather's supper was sitting like lead in the base of my stomach, and Leviticus Lee was tossing about on his bed and moaning, and every now and then, I was sure, I could pick up another mention of gold.

I returned the next day to the place I had buried Lee's hand and examined the thicket. There were tracks, and a few dribbles of blood. That confirmed it: My shot had struck whomever it was that had shot at me.

My heart was in my mouth, I scoured the area for a body. I didn't find one. Maybe the wound had been superficial, and whoever it was had just gone home to heal. I hoped so. The urge to get away from this region became all the stronger.

As I was preparing to go, I happened to glance

back up to the place where I had buried the hand. What I saw stopped me cold.

The stones I had laid atop the dirt mound were rolled aside, and, to my shock, the box was dug up and the top pried off. I advanced up and looked, amazed and mystified. There was the hand, unwrapped to the point that it could be identified.

On the ground around was blood. What could it mean?

What else could it mean but one thing? The man I had shot in the thicket must have come back here, even while dripping blood from his wound, and dug up this box to see what was in it. But why? It made no sense.

I thrust the hand back into the box, fist-hammered the top back onto the box, and reburied it by hand. Then I got out of those woods like the devil was nipping my neck.

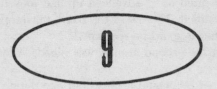

9

The next morning I awakened with a conviction that I had best put aside everything except my original purpose in coming to Arkansas. Only the lure of Minnie had brought me here, but so far I hadn't even looked for her, so distracted had I been with murderous mountaineers, Leviticus Lee, and the Fairweathers.

I ate breakfast as quickly as I could, chilled by the unpleasant glare of Blanche Fairweather and equally chilled by the smile of her husband. The children apparently found me fascinating. I was peppered with questions from the little ones all through the meal, questions about me, questions about Leviticus Lee. The former I wasn't willing to answer, and most of the latter I couldn't. Lee was as much a mystery to me as to anyone.

I excused myself and said I was going into Farleytown this morning to see if my wife might be there. I had deliberately waited until after Robert Fairweather had finished his breakfast and left in the buckboard before I made the announcement, because

I simply didn't want to have to ride into town with him. After I had fetched my jacket and put on my gun belt, I headed toward the door. Blanche Fairweather followed me and called me to a halt outside.

"Mr. Brand, you may be aware that I don't much like having you here," she said.

"Ma'am, you've made that clear enough in every way you could. But don't worry—I'll be gone soon. It was never my intention to impose on your family."

"I know that. I don't fault you for bringing your injured friend here."

"Then what is it you so dislike about me?"

She looked at me from head to toe, like she was trying to figure out where to begin her criticism. "I don't trust you, Mr. Brand. I've always been told I was an overly suspicious soul, and quite possibly that is true. You're a stranger; I don't know who you are or what you've done. For all I know, you and this Leviticus Lee may be on the run from the law. Maybe he got that wounded hand in a holdup, or a gunfight. I don't know—but here you are, among my children, managing to make them think you're the most interesting man they've ever seen . . . a man who comes out of nowhere." She glanced down at my gun belt. "A man who wears a gun."

"A lot of men wear guns when they travel, Mrs. Fairweather."

She ignored that. "Tell me, Mr. Brand: Why have you really come to Farleytown?"

"To find my wife. I've told you that already."

"It's no wife you're seeking. It's gold."

I cocked my head. "Why do you say that?"

"Because of my husband. He's heard something that your partner said, something about gold coins. He believes that you and your partner know the way to the Confederate gold."

"What Confederate gold?"

"Don't play ignorant with me, Mr. Brand. You know exactly what gold I'm talking abut. It's the same gold that my husband made a fool of himself trying to find ten years ago. He became so obsessed with it that he almost destroyed our life together ... but in the end he put all that aside, and became the good man he was born to be. Now you've come, he's changing again. Becoming obsessed with an old myth that I wish to God would just die."

She crossed her arms against the chill of the wind. "Mr. Brand, I would like you to leave this house as soon as you can, and take your friend with you. I'll not be uncharitable and toss him out while he's yet weak from his amputation—but as soon as he's healed, I want you gone."

"I've never had any other intention than that, Mrs. Fairweather." It was odd, but though everything she had said would have seemed prone to make my angry, I didn't feel mad at her. Her rudeness was not without reason; she saw me and Leviticus Lee as threats to the security of her home and the welfare of her husband. I couldn't fault her. "Believe me, you don't want me away from this place any more than I want to be myself." I was thinking of the shooting in the forest, and the oddity of the dug-up hand. The whole thing had spooked me so badly that I didn't feel safe here.

"I'm glad to hear that, sir." She gave me that up-and-down evaluative stare again. "I've seen your kind, Mr. Brand. Trouble follows men like you. I fear it's already followed you into my household."

With that she turned and went back into the house. Her last comments left me a little stunned. Was there really something about me that attracted trouble? Lord knows I couldn't deny that I found more than my share of it, no matter where I went. It was troubling to think that it might not be mere coincidence, that I was some sort of living and breathing magnet for difficulties.

I shook my head. Superstition, that's all that kind of thinking was, and I wasn't a superstitious man. Pulling my coat closer around my collar, I trudged off down the Fairweather's curving drive and toward the road to Farleytown.

Before the day was over, I would be wondering if there wasn't something to be said for superstition after all. By the time I would return to the Fairweather house that day, I would find that, true to Mrs. Fairweather's evaluation, trouble had again followed me.

Here's what happened. I walked into Farleytown and took a look around, thinking that this was surely the ugliest little hamlet I had ever had the misfortune to lay eyes on. Built on a muddy flat where two roads crossed, it was nothing more than a gaggle of buildings that looked like they had been tossed into place out of a giant dice cup. The majority faced each other in two rows. Not even, uniform rows, but haphazard, ragged ones. If you were to hire an artist to paint a portrait of Farleytown in those days, it would have been best to get him thoroughly drunk before handing him his brush and paint board. Only a drunk could properly capture the impression made by this little Arkansas community.

It was easy to pick out Fairweather's big store. It

was the first building on the left when you came in from the direction I was walking. It stood two and a half stories tall, had a long and sagging front porch, and was an interesting place to look at, if not an attractive one. It badly needed a new coat of paint, which is only to say that it fit in perfectly with the rest of the town.

Other than the Fairweather store and a smattering of houses up in the hills in the background, there was nothing but a barber parlor, a smithy (much worse-kept than the one I had operated back in Fort Scott), a shop for wagon and buggy repair, a little log church building up on a knoll behind the smithy, and several saloons. Five, maybe six of them, all lined up. It was a sorry little hamlet—just the kind of place a brilliant intellect like Joben Malan would come with a stolen woman.

That set me to thinking: Why, in all seriousness, would Joben have picked this place to come to? Maybe he had kin here; there must have been something to attract him. I went to one of the saloons, which were already open on the pretext of serving meals—mostly of the liquid variety, I noticed—to ask if there were any Malans around Farleytown.

Entering one of the saloons at random, I found a fat barkeep and a single customer. "Come in and set," the barkeep said. He was chewing a cigar and needed a shave. "What'll you have?"

"Cup of coffee. And a biscuit with jam."

"Make it a biscuit with butter, and you can have it. No jam on the premises."

"Fine."

I talked to the barkeep to gain his confidence, and was surprised to find he already had an idea of

SPECIAL FREE-TRIAL OFFER FOR ALL LOUIS L'AMOUR FANS

- Now – your favorite Louis L'Amour Westerns in handsome hardcover Collector's Editions
- Convenient home delivery
- Return any book you don't want

PLUS – YOURS FREE

Just for looking! Next year's Louis L'Amour Wall Calendar featuring thirteen beautiful four-color scenes from the Old West

NO PURCHASE REQUIRED!

Detach Here. Send no money now, but please do reply today. Thanks!

FREE CALENDAR!
15-DAY FREE
EXAMINATION

Send SACKETT for 15 days free! If I keep this volume, I will pay just
$4.95 – A SAVINGS OF OVER 58% OFF the current low regular
rate of $11.95 plus shipping and handling*. Future Louis L'Amour
Westerns will be sent to me about once a month at the regular rate,
on a 15-day Free Examination basis. I understand that there is no
minimum number of books to buy, and I may cancel my subscription
at any time. The Free Louis L'Amour wall calendar is mine to keep
even if I decide to return SACKETT.

NAME

ADDRESS   APT#

CITY

STATE   ZIP

41400   IL7

**SAVE OVER
58% OFF!
FIRST VOLUME
ONLY
$4.95**

MY NO RISK GUARANTEE:

There's no obligation to buy. The FREE
calendar is mine to keep. I may
preview SACKETT for 15 days.
If I don't want it I simply return
the book and owe nothing. If I
keep it, I pay only $4.95
(plus shipping and handling)*.

*(and sales tax in NY and Canada)

Stake your claim to this FREE book offer.
Send for your Collector's Edition of SACKETT,
and your FREE Louis L'Amour wall calendar.
Try the Louis L'Amour Collection with no
obligation. See details inside.

DETACH HERE BEFORE MAILING

BUSINESS REPLY MAIL
FIRST CLASS MAIL   PERMIT NO. 2154   HICKSVILLE, NY

POSTAGE WILL BE PAID BY ADDRESSEE

The Louis L'Amour
Collection

Bantam Doubleday Dell Direct
PO Box 956
Hicksville NY 11802-9829

NO POSTAGE
NECESSARY
IF MAILED
IN THE
UNITED STATES

who I was. Apparently the arrival of myself and Lee at the Fairweather house had generated lots of interest around Farleytown. It wasn't really surprising, when I thought about it further. Probably very little happened around here; it wasn't unlikely that two newcomers arriving under unusual circumstances was the biggest event to hit Farleytown in a year.

"Tell me, sir, do you know anybody of the surname 'Malan' living around here?"

The barkeep screwed up his face, thinking. At the same moment, a pistol blasted just behind the saloon, so loud it made me jump. The barkeep didn't even blink.

"Malan, Malan . . . nope. No Malans I know of."

Another pistol blast.

"Well, have you by any chance seen a couple, a man and woman, both fine-looking, hereabouts lately?"

"Can't say as I have."

The pistol fired again, and this time a hoot and holler, raised collectively by several male voices, followed.

"What's going on back there anyway?" I asked.

"Paul Merrick's back, that's all."

"Paul Merrick? Who's that?"

"Local fellow, son of Bass Merrick. Richest durn man in the county, Bass Merrick is. He's foreign too. Australian."

"No joshing? I never saw a live Australian before. Nor a dead one, for that matter. What's the shooting about?"

"Paul Merrick likes to bury hens up to the neck and practice his pistol shooting on the heads. That's his way of letting off steam. He's been off in Texas somewhere the last couple of weeks, probably just drinking and running around with the women; that's the sort of things he likes to do. He just got back in town this morning."

I finished my coffee and left money on the bar. Heading out, I circled around the block to see the shooting party in the back; there was no shorter route, the saloons all being built in a row with shared side walls, no alleys between.

It was my fault that I didn't notice that my point of emergence was just the place this Paul Merrick had buried his chickens. Just as I circled around the last building, another shot blasted, and a chicken buried right at my feet was called to whatever afterlife awaits feathered creatures. A splatter of chicken blood stained my pants leg. I yelped and danced to the side, probably rather comically, then let out another yell when I saw the blood on my leg. In the confusion of the moment, I thought it was me who had been shot.

The gaggle of men gathered around Paul Merrick—a rather short but well-featured young man of about my own age—reacted with a couple of seconds of stunned silence, followed by an explosion of laughter.

"Well, gent, have I given you a fright?" Paul Merrick called in an accent unlike any I had ever heard. It reminded me of a Britisher's talk, but with a difference—the typical Australian accent, later experience would teach me.

I was just then making sense of what had happened. My temper flared. "You'd best watch where you're shooting, fool! If you'd have hit me, I'd have made you eat that pistol."

Merrick put on an exaggerated expression of fear.

"Whooo! Listen to him, gents! It appears I've roused up a mad hedgehog!"

"Hey, I know who that is," one of Merrick's companions said. But Merrick wasn't listening; he had already lifted his pistol. I don't think he would have done it had he seen that I also had a pistol; my coat hung over the gun belt, however, and he must have assumed I was unarmed.

"Let's see that dance again," he said, and fired.

The bullet struck squarely between my feet and made me prance again. Merrick laughed heartily, and repeated the procedure. Growing furious, but unwilling to draw my pistol at the moment for fear he would shoot me in response, I took two steps toward him; he again raised his pistol, aimed, and squeezed the trigger.

Click.

Good—his pistol was empty. He had failed to count his prior shots. He gaped at the pistol as I strode up, drew back my fist, and pounded him in the mouth. He fell back with a grunt, tried to sit up, groaned, and fell back again. His mouth was bleeding.

Only then did I realize what I had done. My attack on him had been purely reactive, spurred by his treatment of me. I looked around at the startled men around me.

"We don't want no trouble," one of them said, waving his hands rapidly with palms facing me.

"Neither did I," I replied. "You saw what he was doing with that pistol, and that I did nothing to prompt it."

"We saw it, sure did. Hey, you're that fellow what come in with the old man who lost his hand over at the Fairweather house, ain't you?"

"Never mind who I am. Tell me how this fellow's going to react when he gets his sense back."

Paul Merrick moaned and put his hand to his mouth. He took it away again and studied the blood. "I'm bejiggered if you didn't break my lip!" he said. "I ought to kill you for that!"

He dug into his pocket and pulled out cartridges. Opening the cylinder of his pistol, he spilled the empties onto the ground and started to reload.

I threw back my coattail, pulled out my own pistol and leveled it at him. "I'd stop right there, if I was you."

He seemed surprised when he realized I was armed, but kept right on loading.

"I said to stop that! Don't make me shoot!"

He didn't stop, and I was left with a choice: Shoot him or knock him cold. The latter seemed the best option. I brought up my Colt and clunked it down on his skull even as he slammed the sixth cartridge into place.

Paul Merrick fell to the side, flopped out on the ground like a scarecrow with its supports kicked out.

I holstered my Colt. "Where does he live?"

The others had scattered back for some distance when Merrick began loading his pistol. Now they closed in again. "He lives just over that hill yonder. Big old house. But I wouldn't go there, if you're thinking that way. His father, he might just shoot you down for this."

"Don't talk foolish," another said. "Bass Merrick would probably pay this feller for keeping his boy from committing a murder."

I bent over and picked up Merrick, hefting him across my shoulder like a feed sack. The effort made my head hurt; it will still tender from the blows it had received in recent days.

"Whatever Bass Merrick thinks about it, I'm taking this one home," I said. "I want to make sure my side of this gets told right."

They watched me haul him off, and I think it impressed them. If so, good. Maybe none of them would try his own hand at getting the best of me, if I came across strong and fearless.

In truth, I was low about what had happened. Once again I had come looking for Minnie and found only troubles. Blanche Fairweather's assessment of me seemed all too accurate. As I strode down the road, looking for the Merrick house and generating laughter from those who saw me, I wondered if life was ever going to get back to normal again.

There it was, a large house, built at the far base of the hill that I had just passed around. It was only one story tall, but sprawling, and with a low-peaked roof. I would see pictures later of similar houses in Australia. Bass Merrick had built his house to remind himself of his homeland.

By now I was puffing from the exertion of carrying my human load, a load which was beginning to come to and groan a little.

Ahead, the big front door of the house opened and a broadly built man emerged. His face was a thicker version of Paul Merrick's; his accent, too, was like Paul Merrick's, but thicker.

"Well, which is it: drunk or shot?"

Odd, how he asked that. It was a question idly presented, as if the answer hardly mattered.

"Neither one. Just pistol-whipped."

"By whom?"

"By me, and with good reason."

The big man looked at me, and a smile spread like melting butter across his face. He threw back his head and laughed.

"My friend, come in and dump that load you carry. My name is Bass Merrick, and I'd like to make your acquaintance."

"You're not going to shoot me for this?"

"Shoot you? Why the bloody devil should I shoot you? I know my son well enough to know that any problem he has, he has brought upon himself."

"He was shooting between my feet to make me dance."

"No! I thought he was shooting chicken heads."

"That too."

I carried Paul Merrick into the house and dumped him on a sofa. He groaned, rolled off onto the floor and sat up.

"Father!" he said when he looked up, bleary-eyed. "How did I get—"

"Shut up, stand up, and fetch me and my friend a beer," Bass Merrick said. "It'll be the first useful thing you've done this day, without a doubt."

10

At the Fairweather's supper table that night I suggested that perhaps I should find a room in town and quit imposing on the family. Blanche Fairweather gave me the most pleasant look I had received from her since my arrival, but Robert Fairweather waved his hands and shook his head and said that he wouldn't even consider it. "You and Mr. Lee are our guests for as long as you remain," he said. His wife let out a telling sigh, rose, and went to the kitchen to replenish the bowl of boiled potatoes.

"I'm sorry you didn't find your wife today," Robert Fairweather said. "Are you sure she came to Farleytown?"

"Not really. It's just a name that the bird was saying; I figured it had picked it up, hearing her talk about it."

"It's a bad thing, husbands looking for straying wives, and all of it laid out in front of decent children to make them ask questions they shouldn't," Blanche said icily. She had returned with the refilled bowl in time to hear my comment.

"Hush, dear," Fairweather said. "Such things happen even to good folk." Then to me: "I heard in the store today that Wilt McCoy's family has a couple of visitors, a man and a woman. The McCoys live some miles north of Farleytown. It might be worth investigating."

"It might. Thank you, Mr. Fairweather."

"For heaven's sake, call me Robert. Or Bob, if it suits you. 'Mr. Fairweather!' Land's sake!"

"I heard in town that you had a fight with Paul Merrick today," one of the boys said. It made me wince. I had hoped that wouldn't get back to the Fairweathers.

"I heard the same—is it true?" Robert Fairweather asked. From his expression I got the feeling he hadn't wanted this to come up either, probably because he knew it would only make his wife more deadset against me. Now that the subject was out, of course, there was no reason to be reticent.

"I'm afraid it is true. But he was the one who caused it."

Blanche Fairweather let out another loud sigh and clicked her fork a little too loudly on her dish—a wordless comment no one missed.

"Oh, I don't doubt it was Paul at fault," Robert Fairweather said. "Paul Merrick is trouble, trouble. That's all he is. Just trouble."

"I heard that you carried him right back to his house after you knocked him out," the oldest boy said. The admiration in his tone was obvious.

"Well, I figured it best to lay what had happened right on the line, without rumors getting started . . . or Paul Merrick giving only his side of things."

"How did Bass Merrick receive you?"

"Well, I was surprised. He seemed to think it was funny. He made his boy serve me beer."

Blanche piped up sternly: "We don't drink beer in this house, and I don't think it fitting to discuss that foul beverage before the little ones!"

"Land's sake, dear, the little ones see saloons in town every day. There's no reason to pretend such things don't exist," Fairweather said. It was getting to be a pattern: Blanche talking like I was vermin, and Fairweather contradicting her and making it seem I could do no wrong even if I tried. I was more sure than ever that he saw me as a means of potential gain; nothing else could account for him buttering me up all the time, like he did.

"So he treated you well, did he?" Fairweather said to me. "That is odd. But not surprising. There's nothing about Bass Merrick that isn't odd, in my opinion. I don't tend to trust many who come from foreign shores."

"Just who is he anyway?" I asked. "He had little to tell me about himself except that he had just come home from a business trip to Missouri, and that his son had just come home too. Not from business, but from running around in Texas and doing"—I glanced at Blanche's dour face—"doing things he shouldn't."

"Bass Merrick is the richest man within three hundred miles or more," Fairweather said. "He made his fortune in the Ballarat gold fields, married himself an Arkansas girl, and moved here. His wife died shortly after they settled, and he and his son have been on their own ever since. Bass Merrick doesn't so much work as look out for his investments—cattle in Texas, some mining interests here and there, and meat packing up in Missouri. As for his son, he doesn't work at all. He doesn't make money, or invest it. He just spends it. Gambling, women, liquor, you name it."

"Hardly fit talk for the table," Blanche muttered. Fairweather ignored her.

"Merrick must be a smart man, to have made it that rich while he was still young," I said.

"Oh, he's smart, no doubt. A clever fellow. Not everyone likes him, but I've never had any problems. He provides me lots of business, I don't mind saying."

One of the sons spoke. "And Bass Merrick has looked for the Confederate gold too, just like Father has."

Robert Fairweather looked at his son as if the boy had committed some impropriety on the level of pointing out that a guest had a glass eye or six fingers on one hand. His sharp glance shifted my way and softened into a look of embarrassment.

"That might not be the best subject for the moment, eh, Mr. Brand?"

"No, no, it's fine with me. In fact, it gives me a chance to ask what this Confederate gold is supposed to be."

Fairweather's eyes broadened in surprise. "You don't know?"

"No, I don't."

Instantly his eyes narrowed again, and now his expression was one that said, *Of course you know.*

"I'll tell you what the Confederate gold is," Blanche said. "It's an idle tale told by fools and believed by the same."

Fairweather responded angrily, "Blanche, it's your own husband you insult when you say that. You know I've looked for the gold my very self. And so has Bass Merrick, and you certainly can't call him a fool."

"No, because he's had the sense to declare that he

no longer believes in that old tale. He's learned to tell when something's real and when it's make-believe."

"I haven't looked for that gold for years now, Blanche," Fairweather said. He paused. "That's not to say it isn't real. It may be that no one has known the right place to look." His glance came my way. "At least, nobody who's come along before now."

I ignored the obvious implication. "Tell me this story," I said. "I ain't lying when I say I don't know it."

Fairweather's smile wasn't his usual gushing beam, but a sort of smirk that indicated he was willing to go along with the game he obviously believed I was playing. "All right, I'll tell you.

"Back in 'sixty-two, in the midst of the war, there was some Confederate payroll money, in gold coins, buried somewhere in the hills around Farleytown. There were some soldiers, six, seven of them, charged with delivering the gold to the payroll officer in a big Rebel camp a few miles south of town. Along the way they ran into a Union patrol, and shots were fired. Some of the gold couriers were killed, but three survived. They ran from the Federals, way back into the hills, and stashed the gold into a crevice somewhere at the base of one of the cliffs hereabouts. And there it lays to this day. Nobody ever came back to claim it."

"How much gold was there?"

"I've got no idea. Must have been plenty, though. It was to be pay for a lot of men."

"Is there any proof this is true?"

"None at all," Blanche said before her husband could answer.

Fairweather frowned at her. "There have been many intelligent people who have believed the story of the Confederate gold. Take Bass Merrick, for instance."

"Or Parker Cuthbert," Blanche said. The children laughed; Fairweather turned red.

"He's an exception," he said. "Blanche, are you trying to make me look a fool before our guest?"

"It's not me who believes in old tales of lost gold," she said. "Now, pardon me, dear, I'm going to start washing up these dishes. Girls, I need your help."

Fairweather, now in a bad mood, shooed the boys away from the table as well. "Now, maybe we can talk without being interrupted," he said.

"Who's this Cuthbert?"

"Oh, just a local idiot and drunk, that's all. He came to Farleytown about five years ago, acting mysterious and like he was something special. He headed out into the hills, and three days later he was back, wailing that 'his' gold was gone. It wound up that Cuthbert claimed to be one of the soldiers who buried the payroll, you see, and he declared it had been moved from its proper place."

"So what happened to him?"

"He went off his rocker, as they say. Took to drinking and brawling and trying to hurt people, until folks finally left him alone. He lives in a little cabin outside of town now, a place he rents from Bass Merrick, by coincidence. He works odd jobs, takes whatever folks will hand him out, and still pokes around the hills, looking for his gold. He's insane. No question about it."

"But I gather you believe in this gold too."

He looked at me, grinning slyly. "One can't know what a man believes by looking at him . . . can he?"

I was about to say to him that he had it all wrong, that I really didn't know anything about any gold, and hadn't come to Farleytown to find any lost treasure but Minnie Brand. But I didn't get it said, for just as I opened my mouth I remembered Leviticus Lee's raving about gold coins, and wondered if maybe, just maybe, he might really know something about this old legend. Something true. Something that could lead to the gold.

In the interim during which this came to my mind, Fairweather leaned back and said. "You know, I saw Parker Cuthbert today, coming out of one of the saloons. They give him food on 'credit,' which in his case means they give him food, no payment expected. And you know what? He was limping, really bad, and had a bandage around his leg. I turned to a fellow there with me—buying some flour, he was—and I said, 'What happened to Parker Cuthbert's leg?' And you know what he said? He said that the old fool had gotten himself shot somehow. Stealing chickens, no doubt. Old Doc Ruscher had to dig a bullet out of his leg. On 'credit,' of course."

Fairweather laughed, but I didn't. I suppose I must have had an odd expression, for he looked at me and asked if I was all right.

"Fine, fine." I rubbed my belly as if it were bothering me. "Just a little sour stomach hit me a-sudden, that's all."

"Blanche's food will do that to you," he said.

"I'll go up and lie down a minute until I feel better," I said.

I was glad to be up and away from that table, so he couldn't see that I was trembling. The tale about Parker Cuthbert and the wounded leg had told me something important: I knew now who it was who had shot at me while I was burying Leviticus Lee's hand, and who I had put a slug into in return.

Furthermore, I was beginning to suspect I knew why.

11

When I entered the upstairs room to sleep, the first thing I noticed was that the parrot's cage was open and Bird was gone.

Lee was sitting up in bed, looking pale and wan as with his single hand he thumbed through a picture book obviously borrowed from one of the younger Fairweather children.

"How you faring, my friend?" I asked him.

"Tolerable." His voice sounded weak. "Trying to get used to the notion of going the rest of my days with only one paw. How's a man supposed to wash one hand? How's he supposed to carve up his steak, or dig with a shovel, or do most anything else, for that matter?"

"I don't know; I got no experience with anybody one-handed, up until now." I shuffled my feet. "I feel responsible. It was for my sake you got into that row with those mountain men and got your hand shot."

"I helped you because I wanted to, so don't worry about it. I ain't. I can think of worse things to lose than a hand."

Grinning, I said, "You're a remarkable man, Leviticus Lee."

"Not 'specially so. Not that I can see."

"Well, I sure owe you one. By the way, you been keeping straight our story about how you came to be hurt?"

"Yes, yes—I ain't stupid, you know. It was an accident, all your fault, so on and so on." He grinned weakly. "You know, that Fairweather woman, she questioned me right close about it. I don't think she likes me. Or you either."

"I know it. She thinks we're bad men, I reckon." I waved toward the empty cage. "What happened to Bird?"

Lee looked sheepish. "I turned him loose out the window, Mr. Brand, and I'm ashamed to admit it, for I know it was your wife's critter, not mine." Despite what we had gone through together, I was still Mr. Brand to him, and would remain so perpetually. "That chattering was getting on my nerves, and I just sort of up and did it without really thinking it through. It was durn hard, doing it one-handed. Don't worry—I'll pay you for the bird, soon as I can."

"When will that be? When you find the lost gold?"

My words brought a pall into the room. Lee looked at me in utter silence for almost ten seconds.

"What are you talking about?" he asked at last, even though it was far too late now to play ignorant. His silence had already spoken his full understanding of what I had said.

"About the legend. The old story. The Confederate payroll gold they say is buried in a crevice somewhere around here."

Again he looked at me for a long time, his facial muscles in motion beneath his skin, reflecting the working of his mind. At length the subtle twitching stopped and he looked at me in a different way, and I could tell he had made up his mind to be open with me.

"How'd you figure it out?" he asked.

"I didn't, really, at least not on my own. And the thing is, there's others who have figured it out too."

"Others?"

"Yes . . . Mr. Fairweather here, for one. I think that's why he's being so charitable to us. He figures we've come for the lost gold, and I suppose he expects he'd be rewarded out of it. Mrs. Fairweather confirmed that to me, in fact. That's why she despises us so. Robert Fairweather, you see, used to look for that gold regular. Apparently it about ruined his marriage until he gave it up at last. And now, since we've been here, he's started thinking about that gold again."

Lee swore to himself, then said, "Well, I had thought I might have raved about that gold some. I'll tell you the truth about that missing parrot, Mr. Brand. It was talking about gold coins, repeating things it must have heard me say. I turned it loose because I was afraid folks would hear him and start figuring things out. I see now I was too late."

"There's somebody besides the Fairweathers and me who've figured it out, I'm sorry to say. That's the main reason I'm talking to you about this; it's not just me poking into your business. You see, Mr. Lee: I buried your hand like you had asked."

"I'm obliged. A man hates to have his parts just tossed out."

"While I was burying it, somebody took a shot at

me. I think it's likely a local man named Parker Cuthbert who did it, a fellow they say is a drunk and an idiot who's been looking for the lost gold for several years now. He was seen in town with a wound in his leg afterward. That's why I think it's him."

"But why would he shoot at you?"

"By the time I buried that hand, word about us had gotten out, names and all. One of Fairweather's boys had talked us up big in town when his pap sent him to fetch the doctor. I figure this Cuthbert heard that Leviticus Lee was in town, and knew somehow that you would know where the gold is hidden. Maybe he even thought you had already recovered it. So when he saw me leaving the house with a shovel, he figured it was the gold I was burying, or digging up, one or the other. Robert Fairweather, by the way, had the same notion, and seemed mighty disappointed when he found out it was just your left paw I was putting away."

Then I told Lee the story of all that had happened, how the shot had been fired, and how I had returned a shot of my own. I told him about the blood on the ground, of how the buried hand had been dug up.

"That's some tale!" he said.

"Mr. Lee, I ask you to tell me straight out: Do you really know where the Confederate gold is hidden?"

This time, the pause was longer before he answered. "Yep. I sure do."

"Let me throw another guess at you, and you tell me if I'm right: Were you one of the soldiers who buried the gold in the first place?"

"I was."

"Then tell me this: Is it possible that this Cuthbert knows you were one of those soldiers?"

Lee shook his head. "No, and that's what throws me. I never heard of no Cuthbert before. The only men ever alive who knew where the gold was buried was the three of us who hid it. And the other two are dead."

"How'd that happen?"

"The war killed one of them, two days after we hid the gold. His name was Hargrove, Van Hargrove, a boy from Alabama, if I recall aright. The other was Pete Revett, out of Georgia. He lived out the war, but he was killed right after the peace was made. Murdered, before he ever got home. Some kind of brawl in a barroom, I think."

"The war's been over a lot of years now, Mr. Lee. Why did you wait so long to come after the gold?"

"Because up until now, I ain't been free to come after it." He looked somber, and licked his lips. "I was in prison in Missouri up until a few weeks ago. I had me a fight, you see, over a woman. It was right after I got out of the service. The other fellow died. The details ain't important. Suffice it to say that I escaped the noose, but not the bars. I was locked away for more than twenty long years. But the whole time I was in, I knew I'd come get my gold, just as soon as they set me free. That's all that kept me going. All I had to live for."

"*Your* gold?"

"It ain't nobody else's, is it? That gold was the property of the Confederate government. You may not have noticed, but the Confederate government ain't around no more."

I sat down, taking it all in and letting it settle in

my mind. It was a remarkable tale, but I couldn't figure out where, or how, Cuthbert worked into it.

"You sure you didn't know any Parker Cuthbert?"

"Never heard the name before in my life."

"Well, he must have heard yours. Somehow he knows you can lead him to the gold. He must want it awful bad, to have shot at me."

Lee settled back. He looked very tired and pale. He moved the stump of his hand and made a face of pain. "It hurts," he said. "I can feel them shot-off fingers hurting, even though there ain't a hand there no more."

"I've heard of that happening," I replied. "You want some more of that laudanum?"

"No, no. It turns me into a slug who can't do nothing but lie and stare at the ceiling. And I got to get out of this bed, quick. My gold's out there, waiting for me." He looked at me closely. "Mr. Brand, I like you. You've stuck by me, and I intend to reward you for it. Just as soon as I get that gold."

The words sent excitement all through me. I didn't like to admit it to myself, but I was just as gold-hungry as Robert Fairweather, whose ill-concealed and self-serving lust for gain was so repellent.

Yet my self-respect demanded that I not accept Lee's offer—at least, not too readily. "You saved my life, Mr. Lee. You don't owe me a thing—it's me who owes you."

"If I want to share my gold, I can share it," he said. "I want you to benefit from my good fortune. You don't think I'd shut you out, do you? When I get my gold, you'll find fortune smiling. I'll make you well-off enough that your Minnie will come running back to your arms."

I grinned and nodded—and wondered if he really meant what he said. Maybe he was telling me this because he secretly mistrusted me, figuring that if he didn't make me some sort of bribing promise, I might force him to find the gold and then take it for myself. That poisoning thought led to another, and I began to mistrust Lee: What if he sneaked out when I wasn't about and got his gold on his own, and I never got a bit of it?

Not that I had any kind of claim on that gold anyway. If I had been thinking clearly, I would have recognized that. But that's the problem with gold: It keeps you from thinking clearly.

As I said before, gold is a curse. As it brings fortune, it brings misfortune in greater share; as it brings satisfaction and security, it also brings envy and lies and mistrust. Before much more time had passed, I would see all this. At that moment, however, I saw none of it. The promise of a share of the Confederate gold had a gleam so bright it blinded me to all else.

That night the Fairweathers' dogs sent up a racket in the yard. I awakened, oddly tense. Leviticus Lee was deeply asleep; at my insistence he had taken another dose of the liquefied opiate Dr. Ruscher had given him, and wouldn't waken for a long time.

I'm ashamed to confess, even this many years after the fact, as to the real reason I had insisted he take the laudanum. It wasn't out of a charitable desire to ease the pain of his amputation. It was because I knew that as long as he was in a doped stupor, he couldn't rise in the night and get the gold without me.

I rose and went to the window. The night sky was clear, giving me a decent view across the yard. I saw one of the hounds run across, baying. Then something else moved, over near the trees. I caught only the briefest glimpse before it was gone.

It might have been a dog, a cat, a raccoon, or any other type of critter, based on what little I had seen—just motion in the darkness. But I knew what kind of critter it really was: a man, watching the house.

Parker Cuthbert, surely, keeping watch to make sure that Leviticus Lee and his partner didn't sneak out under cover of darkness and take away the gold he lusted for.

It made me furious. I hated Cuthbert right then, a man I had never really seen, and wouldn't know if I met him on the boardwalk. He was a threat, a danger. For a few dark moments I actually wished the shot I had put into him as he hid in that thicket had entered his head instead of his leg.

Never had I entertained a more evil way of thinking—and the worst of it was that I was so taken with gold lust right then that I didn't even notice it was evil.

When I descended for breakfast the next morning, Leviticus Lee was still soundly sleeping. At the table, Robert Fairweather asked me if I was planning to go today to see if the two guests of the McCoy man he had mentioned the day before were Minnie and Joben.

Why is he so interested? I wondered. Was he eager to get me away from the house so he could go up and pump the location of that gold out of Leviticus Lee?

In less than a second I had that thought, and in

less than two I designed my strategy. "I believe I will,"
I replied. "Can you provide me some directions?"

He smiled, reached into the pocket of his shirt
and handed me a folded paper. It bore a hand-
sketched map.

"I made it last night, before I went to sleep. I figured you'd need it today."

*You really do want me out of the house, don't you?
Trying to weasel your way into my part of the gold,
you two-faced thief! Well, I'll put a stop to your
scheme!*

Bitter though my thoughts were, my face showed
nothing but good humor and pleasantness. "You're
mighty kind, Mr. Fairweather . . . Robert, I mean."

"I'd be halfway inclined to go with you, if I wasn't
so busy today," he said.

"The store's got you tied down, huh?"

"In a way. I'm doing some work on the store's
books today. I always do most of that at home. Lord
knows a man can't concentrate on it down at the store,
with folks in and out."

"I see." Now I was sure I had detected his ploy.
I figured I knew the *real* reason he wanted to stay at
home!

Finishing breakfast under the sullen glare of
Blanche Fairweather, I rose, excused myself, and
headed upstairs. Leviticus Lee was just beginning to
waken. Meanwhile, I felt sure, Robert Fairweather was
downstairs, eagerly awaiting my departure so that he
could come up here and try to prospect my one-
handed partner for the whereabouts of the Confederate gold.

"Yes sir, Mr. Robert Fairweather, you do enjoy
conversation," I muttered aloud. "Blab, blab, blab, all

with that fool smile you think hides so much. Well, my good host, you'll have a bit of trouble having a conversation with Leviticus Lee while I'm away. It's hard to talk to a man who's sound asleep."

I went to Lee's bedside and opened up the bottle of laudanum. Pulling open his mouth, I poured a new dose into him, then pushed up his chin to close his mouth again and make him swallow it. He gurgled and moaned, then settled back into sleep.

"Mr. Fairweather, you just come on in and talk all you want to my good friend here. Just come on in!" I chuckled to myself as I whispered the words.

It was probably the nastiest, sorriest thing I had done in my days, and it only goes to show how bad a turn the prospect of wealth can give to a man's sense of right and wrong.

Heading out to the barn, I fetched and saddled my horse, then began the ride toward the McCoy place. Even though finding Minnie was my goal, my mind was too full of Confederate gold, and of dark satisfaction at the clever trick I had played on Robert Fairweather, to leave much room for thoughts about her.

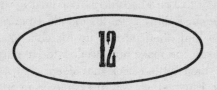

12

Fairweather's map was easy to follow, and I came to within view of the McCoy house very quickly. There I stopped, growing nervous. If Minnie was truly here, how would she react to seeing me? And what about Joben? Would he try to fight to keep her?

My thoughts were interrupted by a loud, feminine wail. On the tail end of that came an angry voice, a man's voice. Both the wail and the voice were familiar—and it sounded to me as if Minnie was in distress, and that Joben was causing it.

My protective husbandly instincts took over at once. Spurring my horse, I galloped up to the front of the house, dismounted even while I reined in, and stomped to the door.

It opened before my hand could reach the latch, and Joben Malan came stomping out, his face red and furious. Minnie was wailing in the background.

When Joben saw me, he staggered back like he had seen a walking corpse, and tripped on the threshold. It landed him on his rump, and from that posture he stared up at me with his mouth open.

"Enoch?" he said. A smile started to creep across his face, then he chuckled. "Enoch, have you come to take her back?"

Minnie, invisible to me somewhere inside the house, stopped her squalling. "Who are you talking to, Joben?"

Joben stood, his face so joyous you would have thought I had just reprieved him from the execution dock. I lifted my hand to shake a fist in his face, but he grabbed the hand when it was only halfway up and started shaking it vigorously.

"Bless you, Enoch Brand, you're a true friend. I never been so glad to see a man, and that's no lie. Hallelujah! Glory be!"

I was so confused now that all my anger was gone. It was me left standing with mouth open and an idiotic expression, worthy of Joben himself, on my face.

"Lord save us, that woman can harp on a man worse than anything! She's like a gnat in your ear that you can't get a pinch on, you know what I mean? God bless you for coming to take her back, Enoch. God bless you!"

"Joben, were you hitting her?"

"Hitting her? Oh no, Enoch, no sir. I just lost my patience and hollered at her. That was enough to get her started crying and fussing. That's all it takes with her."

I couldn't dispute him. My own experience with Minnie had been the same. The woman did go to pieces at the slightest provocation.

"Enoch, how did you know where to find us?"

Joben asked. "I was ready to haul off toward Tennessee just to take her back to you."

"Joben, I asked you who that was you're talking to!" Minnie yelled again.

"It was the parrot," I told him. "It kept saying 'Farleytown.' As best I could figure, it must have picked it up hearing you and Minnie talking about it."

"You're a smart man, Enoch. I never would have figured that out."

"Enoch? Did you say that was Enoch out there?" Minnie said.

"It's me, Minnie!" I yelled in over Joben's shoulder.

"Enoch! Oh, Enoch, thank the Lord you're here! It's a miracle, that's what it is!"

"I see she's not been happy with you any more than you were with her," I commented to Joben. "Now let me ask *you* a question: Why did you bring her to Farleytown, of all places?"

"Relations. some of my mother's people are here—this is their house, though they ain't present at the moment. They went into town yesterday and ain't come back. It was Minnie's fussing what drove them off, I think. Drove them right out of their own home! Lord, she's a nagging thing! Pretty, but hellacious, downright hellacious."

"Well, I figured it must be relatives, though I looked for them under the Malan name. I never thought about your mother's side of the family."

As I was saying this, Minnie was pushing past Joben and rushing to me. She came into my arms and put a big, wet kiss onto my lips. "Enoch, take me away. Take me back to Fort Scott."

"I can't do that, Minnie."

"Can't do . . . what? You've stopped loving me, Enoch? Is that it? Oh Lord, take my soul, just take it on to glory now!" She began bawling again, all the louder.

"I expect even the Lord would want you to calm down some before you were fit to take to glory or anywhere else," I said. "Further, he might have a few things to say to you about the way you've done your husband. You got no idea all I've been through trying to find you, Minnie. No idea at all. But hush and listen to me. I forgive you for running out on me. I forgive you for taking up with old poop-for-brains here. He's a good-looking man, after all. What I meant a minute ago was that I can't take you back to Fort Scott. It's Tennessee we'll go to."

"Tennessee . . ." She choked down a sob and tried to pull herself together. I handed her a handkerchief and she swabbed the various exudings that emotion had produced all down her face. "Tennessee. You're going to make a hayseed out of me, ain't you! Well, it's my lot. My punishment. I was wrong to run out on you, Enoch. I'll not do it again."

Oh, if only I could have believed that. But I didn't want to wrangle with her over that kind of thing right now. "You were wrong, but like I say, I forgive you. Now, let's get your things together. I'm taking you back to Farleytown to meet some folks who've been kind to me."

"You're a good man, Enoch Brand. A good man," Joben Malan said. "May heaven's blessing be upon you."

I told him to shut up, and he did.

*   *   *

We took a slow pace heading back toward Farleytown. It was good to be with Minnie again, and she seemed truly glad to have me back, despite her consternation over the renewed prospect of having to become a Tennessean. Not far from the place we had left Joben, we tethered the horse and walked together in the woods. Her touch was soft and gentle; I knew now why I loved her so, and why I was willing to forgive her again and again. We found a hidden, mossy place and sank down into it. It was a long time before we got up again.

When we were at last back on the road, most of the day had passed. I had totally forgotten my fears that Robert Fairweather was trying to get me away from the house so he could find out the location of the gold from Leviticus Lee. For one thing, Fairweather had proven truthful in what he had told me about the McCoys' visitors; it apparently hadn't been a mere ruse to get me out of the way, as I had thought. For another, I had Minnie again, and that seemed so marvelous that the gold hardly seemed to matter anymore. I had gone from being a fool for gold and back to being a fool for love.

Minnie didn't talk about her days with Joben Malan until we were on the road again. "He was a hard man to live with, Enoch," Minnie said as she clung to me. We were riding double in my saddle. Her meager bag of the personal possessions she had taken with her when she ran off with Joben swung from the saddle horn. "He had no patience with me, none at all. He wouldn't give me nothing I wanted, wouldn't treat me kind and gentle like you always have."

"Maybe you'll see me in a better light from now on," I said. "I'm a bird in the hand to you, Minnie. But you've never been satisfied with that. You're always casting your eyes into the bushes."

"Not no more, Enoch. I'll never even look at another bird in the bush, no matter how pretty he is."

Life hands everyone a few particularly ironic moments, and this was one of mine. Just as Minnie spoke, who should appear on the road in front of me except Paul Merrick himself. He had a rifle slung casually across the crook of his arm, and wore a big grin. He stood with feet firmly planted and spread, and it was clear his intent was to block our path and stop us. He looked very strong and striking and dangerous, and— wouldn't you know it—with Minnie just having pledged to keep her eyes off bush birds, it was the roadside bushes that Paul Merrick had emerged from.

I felt her pull back behind me, and heard her say "Oh!"

"Hello, Mr. Brand," Paul Merrick said in his Australian tones. This elicited a second "Oh!" from Minnie. "Fancy that we should meet like this, out on the road with nobody around." He glanced right and left. "Well, almost nobody."

From the bushes emerged two more men, both of them young. They carried shotguns and looked nervous, one far more so than the other. Obviously they were cronies or hirelings of Paul Merrick.

"What do you want, Merrick?" I asked. "If you're angry because of me trouncing you, you know you brought it on yourself."

"That? Oh, that's forgotten and done, Mr. Brand. It was your victory, and I congratulate you for it. It's no bleeding revenge I'm after, my friend. It's gold."

Minnie said "Oh!" a third time, then gouged me.

"What gold?" she whispered sharply into my left ear. "You've got gold?"

"I don't know what you're talking about," I said to Paul Merrick.

"Don't feed me nonsense, my good friend! You're wasting my time and yours. We both know what I'm talking about. You see, after my little round with you, I asked around a bit. I heard that you came into town with an old codger name of Leviticus Lee. Well, that name might not ring many bells in many minds, but we Merricks, we know some things the average man don't. My father, you see, researched the story of the Confederate gold very thoroughly. Leviticus Lee was one of the three who were assigned to carry that payroll. Therefore, he was one of the three who hid it— and the only survivor of the bunch, incidentally. He's the only man I know of who could put his hands on that gold."

"I heard there's a man named Cuthbert about who claims to be one if the three," I said. I wasn't pleased by how much Merrick knew, and hoped that mention of Cuthbert might somehow confuse the situation in my favor. At the very least, it might reveal something more about Cuthbert, a man in whom I had great interest. After all, he had shot at me, and I was still sure that had been him poking around the Fairweather house in the night.

"Cuthbert? Bah! A fraud and a murderer. That's all he is."

"A murderer?"

"That's right. It was Cuthbert who killed Peter Revett, second of the three who hid the gold. He tried to torture Revett into revealing the location of the gold to him, then killed him after he got the information.

But Revett got the last laugh. He lied to him about the whereabouts. It was enough to drive poor old Cuthbert out of his mind. He's a dangerous man, Mr. Brand. He knows nothing of where that gold lies." He shifted the rifle so that now it dangled in his hand. "But Leviticus Lee knows. And by now, maybe you know as well."

"Why should I know such a thing?"

"He's your partner, isn't he? Partners share secrets with one another."

"Who's Leviticus Lee?" Minnie whispered. "And what gold is he talking about?"

"Hush!" I whispered back. Then I spoke to Paul Merrick again. "I don't know where any gold is. If I did, you think I wouldn't have gotten it by now?"

"I hear your partner had an accident and lost a hand. I hear he's been laid up at the Fairweather house. I figure that's delayed you."

"He's laid up, all right. But I still don't know where the gold is buried."

"Ah, but you can find out, can't you! And that's just what you're going to do for me, Mr. Brand. You're going to find me that gold."

"If you want gold, ask your daddy. I hear he mined aplenty of it in Australia."

"My father and I aren't on the best of terms, Mr. Brand. I have a few . . . habits that tend to become expensive. Right now I've got gambling debts, unknown to my father. I intend to keep them unknown. When you find me that gold, I'll have enough to pay off all my debts, live the way I want to live, and stay in my father's good graces—and his will—for as long as it takes."

"You must be a desperate man, to threaten a lone man and his wife," I said.

"Your wife, is it? Well!" Paul Merrick smiled and tipped his hat. "Good day to you, ma'am. Charmed, absolutely charmed."

"Please sir, please, don't hurt my husband!" she pled in fine dramatic style.

"Hurt him? I don't have any desire to do that, ma'am. Why would I hurt a man whose help I need?"

Now, there was a thought! Why indeed? Immediately I climbed down from the saddle.

"Whoa, there, Mr. Brand! I suggest you stop where you are." Paul Merrick aimed his rifle at my midsection.

"Can't stop yet—I ain't finished," I said, walking straight at him.

"You back off!" he yelled. "Back, you jackass!"

"Should we shoot him?" one of Merrick's cronies asked rather desperately.

"No, no, we need him to—" He broke off, realizing what I already had: He could not afford to harm the very man he was counting on to lead him to the Confederate gold.

I reached Merrick and grabbed his rifle. With minimal effort I wrenched it from his hand.

"Paul, we got to shoot him, we got to!" one of the shotgun bearers said.

"I ain't shooting nobody—ain't enough pay in the world to make me do that!" the other said. He laid down his shotgun and walked away into the woods.

I leveled Merrick's own rifle on him. "Tell the other one to drop his shotgun."

Paul Merrick's face was as red as an overheated

furnace. "Drop the . . . no, wait. Aim your shotgun at Mr. Brand's wife."

The man did as he said. I jabbed the rifle muzzle right into Paul Merrick's belly. "Tell him to drop it."

"No. If you're going to shoot me, shoot. Of course, as soon as you do, your wife will die."

"I don't think you've got the guts to do it."

"It's not a question of my courage, Mr. Brand. It's a question of my companion's meanness. He has plenty of it, I assure you. He'll kill her in the flick of an eye."

"Merrick, when this is over . . ." I lowered the rifle and handed it to him. "All right. You win. I'll do what you want. Just let her go."

"I don't think so."

"What did you say?"

"I'm keeping the lovely Mrs. Brand as a guest of sorts. It's an idea that's just come to me. An inspiration of the moment, you could say. I don't know where your wife has come from or how she came to be here, but her arrival is convenient for my purpose. It appears to me that you care deeply for her. So, if you want to continue to have a wife to care deeply about, it is strongly advised that you cooperate."

"I've already told you I'll cooperate. You don't need to threaten my wife to get my help."

"Let's just consider her collateral, or more accurately, insurance. As long as you cooperate, she'll be safe. If you cross me, she'll be dead. That's no bluff, Mr. Brand. You may count on that."

Minnie was white as paper and looked ready to faint off the horse. "Enoch, don't let them take me!"

"You can't do this, Merrick."

"I don't see a thing in the world to stop me. Certainly you won't. Now, get on with you. Go back to Leviticus Lee, and do whatever you have to do to recover that gold. I want it within three days, and you remember, if there is a sign of law, a sign that you've double-crossed me, the lady will be dead."

"I'll remember."

"Good." He began talking rapidly then, his accent and speed making it hard for me to keep up. What he said, boiled down, was that Minnie would be kept in a place I couldn't find. He then gave me directions to an old shack he said stood in a wild region in the mountains north of town, and told me to meet him there by noon three days hence, with the gold. As soon as it was in his hands, he would free Minnie. And most of all, he told me, I should make sure that Bass Merrick learned of none of this. If he did, Minnie would be killed.

Minnie was crying as they carried her off, but it wasn't her usual dramatic, loud cry. It was a soft, sad, fearful weeping. There was no falsehood or pretense about her now. She was truly scared.

And so was I. So scared I could have been sick. The whole situation staggered my belief. With no more to go on than a stray word from a talking parrot, I had followed my footloose wife through the Ozarks, faced more perils within a handful of days than I had ever dreamed I would in my whole life, and then, almost miraculously, found her again. And now she was taken, and in danger, and I wasn't sure I would ever see her again.

They had left my weapons leaned against a tree a good ways off. I waited until they were out of sight, then collected them. Sad and edgy, I headed back toward Farleytown and the Fairweather house.

I wondered what kind of response I would get from Leviticus Lee when he found that I needed to trade his coveted gold for the safety of my wife. The man had languished in a prison for two decades, living for the day he would recover his lost treasure—and here I was, about to take it from him.

And take it I would, by whatever means were necessary. Minnie's life was at stake, and the gold meant nothing to me now beyond being the necessary means of getting her safely back.

My gold fever was cured. The only treasure I wanted now was the one that I had first come to Arkansas to find, and that was my Minnie.

I rode toward the Fairweather house, my heart as heavy as the red sun that drooped on the western horizon.

13

earful and weary, I turned my mount off the road to circle back toward the Fairweather house. As soon as the house was in view, I knew something was wrong.

Robert Fairweather was in the yard, pacing back and forth, talking loudly to his family. It was clear that some sort of argument was under way. The children and Blanche Fairweather were assembled on the porch and silhouetted against the backlight of the windows. Fairweather was waving his left hand like a tent-meeting preacher going strong. His right hand hung stiffly at his side, clutching a rifle.

"Look!" Blanche Fairweather declared as I came into view. She raised a finger and pointed it accusingly. "There's the very man who's brought this trouble upon our household!"

"Blanche, God help me, I demand that you close your mouth!" Fairweather bellowed. I noticed at the same moment that he had a bandage around his right upper arm.

"What's happened here?" I asked.

"Leviticus Lee is gone," Fairweather said.

"Gone? You mean he's run off?"

"No—he's been carried away. Abducted."

"*What?*"

Blanche Fairweather, clearly in no humor to be an obedient wife this night, stepped down from the porch and up to the side of my horse. "It's you who brought that man here, and you who bear the responsibility for the danger that came upon us tonight."

"Blanche, I told you to—"

"Shut up, Robert!" she shouted. "For once, let me have my say!"

I had dismounted by now. She glared at me bitterly. "A man came to our house tonight. He was armed, and forced us to lie on the floor. He took Leviticus Lee away at gunpoint. When Robert tried to stop him, the man shot him in the arm. Shot my husband! And right in front of the children!" Tears rose, but not tears of fear or weakness. These were generated by pure fury.

"Cuthbert?" I asked.

"No. A stranger," Robert Fairweather answered. "And he just grazed my arm muscle here, that's all. The bullet went into the wall."

"Who could he have been?"

"I'd seen him before," Robert Fairweather said. "In town, just in the last month or so, loitering around in front of the saloons. But I don't know him."

"It's you who caused this to happen," Blanche charged again. "I told you that trouble follows you. I've always been able to spot your kind. My own father was one."

"Enoch, do *you* have any idea who it might have been?" Robert Fairweather asked.

"No," I said. "I never knew Leviticus Lee until just before we showed up here. I don't know much about him, or what enemies he might have. Which way did they go?"

"Back to the road, and after that I don't know," Fairweather said. "I was too distracted by this little wound of mine to take notice. But now I'm ready to go after them. That's what I was about to do when you rode up—against my wife's wishes, I should add."

"It's foolishness, Bob," Blanche said. "You're a storekeeper, not a tracker. You should stay here and protect your kin, not go trailing off in the night. Let the constable take care of this."

"She's right about the tracking. We'll never be able to follow them in the dark," I said. A suspicion was starting to roll through my mind. "But there might be a place I can look. It's just a wild guess, but ..."

Without another word I hefted up into the saddle again and rode toward the road, Robert Fairweather yelling for me to stop long enough to tell him what I was doing. I ignored him; there was no reason at the moment to involve him further in this.

A deep fury drove me now, and a deeper fear. Minnie was a prisoner of a dangerous young man, and the only other person who could lead me to the gold that would buy her freedom was a captive as well.

But a captive of whom? I didn't know ... but I had a possibility in mind.

I urged my horse to a trot and headed through the darkness on the now-familiar road to Farleytown, trying to ignore my near-exhaustion.

Bass Merrick's house was dark, except for a couple of rooms at the rear. I dismounted and tethered my weary horse in a hidden place, and approached cautiously, on the lookout for dogs or any other thing that might give me away.

Edging around the house, I approached one of the lighted rear windows, hoping to get a look inside. There was no way I could be sure that Leviticus Lee was here, or that Bass Merrick was responsible for his capture.

But it made sense to me that Merrick might be the one. Paul Merrick's words to me earlier indicated that when I was first at the Merrick house, he hadn't yet learned about Leviticus Lee being in town. Given that, it seemed unlikely that Bass Merrick had known about it either. By now, however, surely he did know, just as his son did. And just as surely, he had also recognized Leviticus Lee's name and realized his connection with the Confederate gold.

I might have suspected Paul Merrick as being responsible for Lee's abduction, except for one thing: Today's encounter on the road, Paul Merrick's demands on me, and the capture of Minnie would have been unnecessary if Paul Merrick had planned to take Leviticus Lee himself prisoner. Further, I had gone straight from the encounter with Paul Merrick to the Fairweather house, and there simply wouldn't have been time for the younger Merrick to plan and pull off Lee's abduction in that brief interim. Besides, Paul Merrick didn't strike me as brash enough to set up as brazen and invasive a capture as that which had taken Leviticus Lee. He seemed more the type to bully people in isolation, and with armed companions, as he had done today to Minnie and me.

Since the Fairweathers had specified that Parker Cuthbert wasn't Lee's captor, that left only Bass

Merrick as a likely suspect. My working theory was
that Bass Merrick had, like his son, come to realize
that Leviticus Lee could lead him to the gold he coveted. But unlike his son, he had decided to go straight
to the source itself, rather than taking the indirect
route of trying to get the gold through me. It was virtually certain that Bass Merrick knew nothing of what
his son had done today; Paul Merrick seemed very intent on making sure his father did not find out what he
was up to.

The window was covered with thick drapes, making it impossible to see inside. I could hear muffled
and unintelligible male voices, but try as I would, I
could not detect if one of them was Lee.

Moving to another window, I had an equal lack of
success. Now I was bewildered. I could hardly knock
on Bass Merrick's door and say, excuse me, but did
you kidnap my partner, and would you mind giving
him back? Nor could I burst in like some dime-novel
hero and free the captive . . . if he was even here.

As I dawdled and wondered what to do, a door
opened around the corner. A rear door was there—and
someone was coming out of it. There were no bushes
immediately at hand to hide me, and no place to go
but back toward the front of the house, or to the
woods at the side.

I opted for the latter, and made a dash that I
hoped would be quick and quiet. On the third step,
however, my foot trod a stick, which snapped loudly. I
lunged forward all the faster, and my other foot caught
the remnant of the same branch and sent me flat onto
my face.

"Hey, hey you there—hold it!"

There was no point in trying to run now. As I

stood, the man who had emerged from the house was upon me, and others were coming out to join him. I brushed myself off as I was surrounded. The fellows reeked of cigar smoke and whiskey.

"Who are you, and what are you doing here?" one asked.

"Where's Mr. Merrick?" I asked.

In one of those cases of appropriate timing, Bass Merrick came out that same rear door. "What's all this, now?" he boomed.

"Got us a fellow who was poking around under the window," my captor said. "Don't know who he is."

"It's me, Mr. Merrick—Enoch Brand."

"Mr. Brand? Well—isn't this interesting! Come down here and join me and my friends. We're in the midst of a ripping good poker game." His tone was friendly on the surface, but sounded threatening and suspicious just beneath.

"I'm afraid I don't have the time or money for a poker game," I said. "Maybe the best thing would be for me to just go."

"No. Come in. I insist."

I didn't want to go in. If in fact Leviticus Lee was a prisoner here, the odds were I would be taken prisoner as well. And then what would happen to Minnie?

"I'd really best be going," I muttered.

"Stay," he said. His hand slid into a pocket and came out holding a derringer. "I'm afraid I have to know why you've come poking around my house in the dark of night."

He had me taken into a back room, then sent the others out and closed the door behind them. Sitting down in front of me, he crossed his legs and toyed with the little pistol. He didn't aim it at me, but neither did he put it away.

"Mr. Brand, I'm not pleased when folks come poking around my place like you were. It makes me want to ask a lot of questions."

"Let me ask you one first, Mr. Merrick. Where is Leviticus Lee?"

He reacted immediately to the mention of the name. His eyes flashed and a little smile danced across his face for a second or two. "Leviticus Lee! A well-known name to me. Had I known at the time you were last here that you are a companion to the good Mr. Lee, I would have found you even more interesting than I did. But why should I know where Mr. Lee is? It's my understanding that he's a guest at the Fairweather house, just like you."

"He was. He's gone now. Abducted."

"Abducted?" He had no smile now. "In what way?"

"Someone came into the house with a gun, forced the family to hold still, and took him off. Robert Fairweather tried to stop them, and took a wound in the arm for his effort."

Merrick seemed intrigued, and mulled over what I had told him. He brightened in quick comprehension. "Aha! So you thought that perhaps I was responsible, and came here to see—is that it?"

"I couldn't help but suspect you. I'm told you have looked for the Confederate gold for a long time. A man with your knowledge of the lore of the gold would know that Leviticus Lee is the key to finding it."

"*Was* the key, you should say. I'm convinced that the gold existed, but that now it's gone."

"Gone?"

"Yes. I've explored these hills, traced down every shred of evidence, poked through every cave. I don't think the gold is here anymore."

I didn't want to hear that. Without the gold I couldn't get back Minnie. "You think it was taken by someone?"

"Maybe. Or maybe the crevice it was hidden in shifted or opened wider, or was flooded out. The gold could have dropped into the very bowels of the earth. If it's here, it's buried so deep now that it can't be found."

"You sound awfully certain. What grounds do you have for being so sure?"

"I'm not sure, really—it's just speculation. Suffice it to say that I don't feel that looking for the Confederate gold is worthy of any more of my time than I've already given it in years past. I gave up that search some time ago. I don't believe that even Leviticus Lee could put his hand on that gold now. And so, you can see, there's no reason I would have bothered to abduct him. What good could he have done me? Besides, I'm no kidnapper. It's not my style."

I didn't know whether to believe him. But certainly I wasn't going to argue with him, with all the proverbial cards in his hand. "But if not you, then who?"

He smiled an almost mysterious smile. "I might suspect my son, but my son is far away from here. He wasn't much happy about the way I 'shamed' him in front of you—that was his word, 'shamed.' He was all huffed up, let me tell you. So he took off back to Texas and his saloon girls and drinking partners."

That's what you believe, I thought. I could tell

him a few things about what his son had really been doing—but I wouldn't, not until I knew he was trustworthy.

"If I were you, I'd investigate a man named Parker Cuthbert. He's something of a town fool, but he also happens to be the person here most obsessed with the Confederate gold. He might know enough to be aware of Leviticus Lee's connection with that gold. And he would be just the kind to pull something like this."

"I've heard of Cuthbert. But the Fairweathers say it wasn't him who came into their house."

"Well, then maybe it was someone he had hired, or promised a cut of the gold."

I hadn't thought of that possibility. It made sense. "I hear that Cuthbert lives in a house you own. Where can I find him?"

"He did live in it. I threw him out three days ago; I doubt the word has spread yet. He hadn't paid rent for five or six months, and local folk said he'd been acting threatening and dangerous lately. I had my fill of him, and gave him the boot."

"So where's he staying?"

"Who knows? For all I know, he's lodging in a cave. I've given a lot of help to that bloody fool, and I don't care about him anymore."

"Will you let me leave?" I asked.

He smiled slowly. "I will. And I hope you find your partner safe and sound. Let me know what happens. I'm as concerned as you are."

I nodded and headed for the door. The others outside gave me uncertain, dark glances, then looked at Merrick as he followed me out. "It's all right," he said. "Give him back his pistol. He can go."

As I rode away from Bass Merrick's house, I did so with several new convictions. One, I didn't trust the senior Merrick any more than the younger one, even though he had let me go. Something in his manner, something in the way he had held that derringer throughout our conversation, something about the overconfident way he assured me there was no gold to be found . . . it just didn't ring convincing.

He had said he was as concerned as I was about Leviticus Lee, yet he offered me no assistance in finding him. And he had taken great pains to make it clear that he no longer had any sort of affiliation with the mysterious Parker Cuthbert.

But I wasn't buying. There was something odd here, something rather sinister. I was glad I had said nothing about what Paul Merrick had done. Let Bass Merrick believe he was really in Texas, at least for now. To have said otherwise would have endangered Minnie.

It was very late now, and I was so weary I could hardly stay in the saddle. I could do nothing more tonight to find Leviticus Lee. In the morning I would have to seek help from Robert Fairweather.

I longed to return to the Fairweather house and get some sleep, but the prospect of facing off with Blanche Fairweather was too much to take. The way I felt, the way I feared for Minnie's safety, I might just lose control of myself and raise a hand against Blanche Fairweather if I had to choke down any more of her bile.

Outside Farleytown I found a barn that stood out of sight of its affiliated farmhouse. I stabled my horse and fed it on some hay. Then I wrapped my coat around myself, lay down on a pile of hay, and immediately fell into an exhausted sleep.

The sound of riders on the nearby road awakened me. Creeping to the wall, I looked out through a knothole. Three horsemen came past. A chill ran through me. Were these incidental travelers—or had Bass Merrick had me followed?

If the latter, at least I had escaped them, for they had gone right past the barn. Lying down again, I resumed my sleep.

14

When I rode into his yard the next morning, Robert Fairweather seemed hardly less agitated than he had been the prior evening. He came running out of his house to meet me. His wife came to the door but did not come out; she looked harshly at me from its shadows.

"Did you find him?" Fairweather asked urgently. "Where did you go? Where is he? Where is he?"

"I don't have him," I replied. "But I think I know who might. The man who captured him could have been working on behalf of Parker Cuthbert."

"Yes, I suppose he could have," Fairweather said after he thought about it a couple of seconds. "I never considered that Cuthbert might have someone else do the dirty part of the work for him. But where did you go last night?"

"On a chase after a wild goose. It's not important. Listen, Fairweather, I came back here for only one reason. I want you to tell me where Parker Cuthbert might go if he wanted to be out of view. He's no longer in his house. Bass Merrick threw him out because he quit paying his rent."

"I didn't know that ... let's see, let me think ..." He rubbed his chin. After a few moments his face brightened. "The old sawmill!" he declared. "That's a likely spot. I know Cuthbert has been known to go there to drink with some of his friends, if you could call them that."

"Tell me how to get there."

"Wait, my friend, wait. I've been thinking, and Blanche and I have been talking. I think we should notify the constable, just as she suggested. This is becoming far too criminal to be handled by regular folk like you and me."

"No," I replied. "No law." I was thinking of Minnie and what might happen to her if word somehow reached Paul Merrick that I had gone to the law. He would be bound to think I had gone to report his kidnapping of Minnie. Paul Merrick surely had eyes all around; if I did anything too peculiar, he would doubtlessly learn of it. Even going to Bass Merrick's house had been risky, but in this case necessary.

Blanche came into the yard now. "See, husband? He fears the law. Why? What does he have to hide?"

I wanted to scream at her, to tell her to shut up and mind her own affairs before she got an innocent person or two killed. But I kept myself calm, took a deep breath, and said, "Please—let me explain. I'm going to tell you something in confidence, and if you betray me, my wife might pay for it with her life."

"Your wife?"

"That's right. Your hunch was right, Robert. My wife was at the McCoy house, just as you had thought—the McCoys turned out to be relatives of

Joben Malan's mother. I went and fetched her away from there."

"Then where is she now?"

"She's been taken captured too, just like Leviticus Lee. But the difference is I know who has her. It's Paul Merrick. He stopped us on the road and took her hostage. The price of me getting her back is finding the Confederate gold for him. If I go to the law, he'll kill her. I'm sure he would." I looked up at Blanche Fairweather. "That's the reason I don't want to bring the constable into this, ma'am. I hope you can understand that."

"God spare us!" Robert Fairweather said. "What a terrible thing!" He stopped, thinking. "Wait a minute—might it not be Paul Merrick who took Leviticus Lee as well?"

"I don't think so," and I explained my reasons for that opinion. "But whoever has Leviticus Lee," I added, "I've got to find him. Without him I can't find the gold and get my wife back. It's not a matter of greed or gain anymore. It's a matter of Minnie's survival."

"I see." Fairweather rubbed his chin again. "My friend, I'm going to help you. I'll get my rifle and head out to the sawmill with you, and if Leviticus Lee is a prisoner there, then by Jove, we'll set him free! I'm not afraid of Parker Cuthbert."

"We still don't know for sure it's Cuthbert," I reminded him. "Nor do we know that Lee is at the old mill."

"No," Fairweather said. "But I can't think of any better options to pursue at the moment. Can you?"

"No." I stuck out my hand, and actually got a lump in my throat. My earlier greed-inspired distrust of the man was gone. He now knew that even if the gold was found, it would have to be paid out in ransom, yet he was still willing to give me aid. I knew then how wrong I had been about the man, and how blind my own greed for the gold had made me. "I accept your help. Right now I'm desperate enough to take help from anyone willing to give it."

Blanche grasped her husband's shoulder and wheeled him around to face her. "You can't get involved in this—it might be dangerous!"

"Blanche, think of Enoch's wife! Good heavens, woman, if it was you in danger, I'd certainly want someone to help me get you back!"

"How do we know he even has a wife? Why have you been so quick to trust him? It's the gold—that's it. You have gold flashing in your eyes again, and it's making you blind. You still think you can get your hands on it. Your duty is to your own family, to your *own* wife, not to this man's—if she even exists!"

"She exists," I said. "And I intend to see that she continues to exist." Looking to Robert Fairweather, I said, "But your wife is right about your duties. I need your help, but I won't fault you if you back out. Just tell where the mill is, and I'll do this alone."

"Nonsense. I'm going with you."

Blanche Fairweather spat toward me. "I hate you!" she said. "Why did you have to come to our house at all? If my husband goes with you, I'll, I'll . . ."

"You'll go inside, say prayers for my safety, and wait for my return," Robert Fairweather said. "My mind is made up, Blanche. I'll hear no more from you about it."

She looked at me with a venomous gaze. "There

may be more than praying that I can do," she said, and stomped back into the house.

"What does she mean by that?" I asked.

"Never mind her—she speaks her mind too freely," Robert Fairweather said. "I'll go get my guns and horse, and we'll be off."

"Robert, I want you know how much I appreciate this, and that—"

"Hush, son," he said. "Time's wasting."

He went about readying for our venture. When he came back out, he handed me my Henry rifle and a couple of leftover breakfast biscuits with tenderloins stuck in them. I had been so wrought up that I hadn't even noticed how hungry I was.

Armed and mounted, and with me gnawing the biscuits, we set out, Fairweather leading the way toward the old sawmill, and—I hoped—to my captured friend Leviticus Lee.

We wound through scraggly, dark forests, under tall limestone cliffs, along streams, up narrow, abandoned roads, and finally reached a rutted, overgrown route that followed the crest of a ridge. I heard a river splashing along somewhere beyond the trees.

"This is the old sawmill road," Fairweather said. "Not many use it now."

I had dismounted and was investigating the ground. "Somebody used it recently," I said. "Take a look."

There were tracks, relatively fresh, of three horses. I followed them on foot a little ways, and then discovered something else. A strip of white cotton cloth, darkened at one side with blood.

"Look at this, Robert," I said. "Looks to me like a piece of bandage."

"Yes . . . just like the one Leviticus Lee had on that stump of his."

"How far to the sawmill?"

"About a mile."

"No one works there now?"

"It's been abandoned for a couple of years. All that's left is the building."

"If Cuthbert or anyone *is* there, will they be able to see us before we come close?"

"Not unless we round the last ridge and enter on the main road. When we get near that point, I suggest we tie our horses and go over the ridge on foot, and approach the mill from the side. That way we can get a good look at what might be going on before they have much chance to see us."

"They have three horses," I said. "Assuming they brought one to carry Leviticus Lee, that means there's only two men involved. Probably Cuthbert and whoever it was who actually came into your house."

We went on. The autumn Ozark countryside was fantastically beautiful, but I hardly noticed it. I wondered what we were riding into.

A new thought came to me. What if someone was being held at the sawmill—but what if it wasn't Leviticus Lee? This might be the hidden place Minnie was being kept.

What then? Would it be wise to attempt a rescue, or would that simply endanger her? Thinking about it made me nervous. I decided to withhold all such judgment making until we knew what the situation truly was.

That mile of travel was the longest I have ever

known. By the time we reached the ridge that Fairweather had mentioned, the relatively few minutes that had passed seemed like hours. We hid the horses, drew out rifles, and looked at each other.

It struck me then what a ludicrous little army we made—a Kansas blacksmith and a small-town Arkansas merchant, going in to rescue a one-handed former convict from a violent, gold-obsessed town drunk. It really did seem rather funny, in a way.

I felt no inclination to laugh.

"Lead the way," I said to Fairweather.

"All right. Up this way here, quiet and easy, would be the best. I suggest we—"

He cut off suddenly, having heard the same thing I had. A yell of pain—a man's yell. The cry was muffled by distance and distorted by suffering, but it sounded for all the world like Leviticus Lee's voice to me.

Funny, how hearing that cry caused us to forget our planned caution. We scrambled up that ridge like berry-picking boys racing each other toward a particularly productive blackberry vine.

Another yell echoed up, this one virtually a scream. No question about it now—that was Leviticus Lee's voice. Obviously he was in great torment.

"Merciful heaven—I think they're torturing him!" Fairweather whispered.

The sawmill, visible when we topped the ridge and hid in the brush to peer over, was a rambling, rough old structure with a roof half caved in and big pieces of the walls missing. It appeared that parts of the building had been cannibalized over its two years of abandonment and used in other structures. We could see no sign of human life, but the evidence of our ears was entirely sufficient.

"There's their horses," I said, pointing toward the rear of the sawmill, where three hobbled horses picked at dried winter grasses.

"I recognize that old sorrel," Fairweather said. "That's Parker Cuthbert's horse."

Another scream came to our ears. It made me wince.

"I wonder what they're doing to him?" Fairweather said.

"Working on that stump of his, I'll bet." The thought of that kind of cruelty made me angry. Good. I would need anger, and every other motivator I could think of, to do what needed doing.

"We got to go down there," I said. "It appears to me the direct approach will be best."

"What do you mean? Just walk in on them?"

"Why not?"

He shrugged. "I can't think of any better plan. If we can surprise them, maybe we can have them disarmed before they can react."

"We'd best split up—you go in the back, and I'll go in the front. Hitting them from two sides would be to our advantage. We'll get down there together, then when you're stationed at the back, I'll bust right in through the front there. Likely that'll fluster them. When their attention is on me, that's when you need to come in. Keep a sharp ear, all right?"

He nodded resolutely. "I'll do it. By Jove, we'll get that poor man out of there."

Leviticus Lee was screaming again, begging them to stop whatever it was they were doing. I heard another voice, yelling just as loudly as Lee's. "You want us to stop? We'll stop when you tell us where that gold is!"

"That's Cuthbert's voice!" Fairweather said.

Lee, his voice tight with pain but defiant in tone nonetheless, shouted back at his tormentor, inviting him to make a permanent trip to the nether regions.

Fairweather I looked at each other, both of us knowing that if Cuthbert was desperate enough torture a man, he wouldn't be likely to give up without resistance.

"It's not too late for you to walk away from this," I said.

He paused, swallowed, blinked. Then he shook his head. "No. Especially not now that I've heard those screams."

"All right. Be careful."

"I will."

"Well, now's the time," I said. "Let's go."

"Let's go," Fairweather repeated.

And we went.

15

I didn't dare allow myself time to think, for if I did, it would lead to hesitation, and hesitation could bring death to me, Fairweather, or Leviticus Lee.

Using brush and trees for cover, I circled down toward the front corner of the big, unpainted building. It was a dark and rather grim-looking structure, two stories tall, with a heavy iron-ribboned jack ladder leading down from the upper saw floor into the river, which ran directly behind the building. The jack ladder, up which logs had once been hauled for sawing, was one of the few items remaining from the mill's active days. The saws and steam engine apparatus to drive them had been removed.

The place was remarkably clean, the slabs and other saw leavings having inevitably been taken for firewood by local folk. What trash there was now was mostly empty bottles tossed down by the drunks who apparently used this as a hideaway. As I carefully made my way among the bottles, making sure not to cause any clinks or breakage to give me away, I won-

dered how many of these emptied containers had been
drained by Parker Cuthbert.

I glanced down the side of the mill and saw
Fairweather moving into position. He darted to the
jack ladder, crouched beneath it, and gave me a brief
wave to acknowledge his success in traveling unseen.

Waving back, I took a deep breath and began
creeping toward the big front door, a double-gated af-
fair that was almost completely closed. Leviticus Lee
was screaming again; the sound came from just inside
the front doors. When I came bursting through, I
would be directly upon them.

I had a certain curiosity to see Parker Cuthbert, a
mysterious and faceless figure so far. I imagined him
as a husky, brutish creature, topped by thick, wild hair
as dark as his squinted eyes. His nose surely was bul-
bous and etched with veins, courtesy of his drinking
habit.

Well, the time had come ... but I hesitated. Now
that the moment was at hand, I didn't feel very heroic.
I forced an image of Minnie into my mind. Only
through Leviticus Lee could I get the gold I needed to
buy her back. Then Lee let out a particularly fearsome
scream, and I made my move.

But just as I was about to lunge through the
opening between the doors, I heard a shout from inside. "Hold it! I've got my gun on you!"

That was Robert Fairweather's voice—what was
he doing in there? He was supposed to enter after me,
not before. Had he misheard something and taken it
for my signal?

Curses, yells, confusion—then a shot, fired just
inside the door. Fairweather yelled, fired back. The
slug came bursting out through the wall not three

inches from my head, sending splinters of wood all over me.

"*Enoch, where are you?*"

Fairweather's cry was desperate. I moved quickly, wheeling and dodging straight through the gap between the doors—and from the corner of my eye caught sight, just as I disappeared, of two riders coming around the ridge that Fairweather and I had come across, and riding onto the grounds of the sawmill. Who they were or why they had come, I didn't know, and there was no time to see.

The scene that met me inside was as confused as I had anticipated, yet the details of it revealed themselves starkly. There was Leviticus Lee, tied down on a large log, with his handless arm stretched out and tied along the length of a board, which served as a splint to keep him from bending his elbow. His bandage had been pulled off, and it appeared that his torture had consisted of pressure being applied by a second board at the point of his wound.

Two men were in motion as I came in, one surely being Cuthbert and the other his assistant. One, a man with a completely bald head and large ears, was diving behind a pile of rotting lumber, taking cover. The other, a tall, thin man with shuck-colored hair, was already positioned behind one of the big poles that supported the rather barnlike building. He fired off a shot from his Remington pistol toward the far end of the mill, then turned when I came in, cussed, and ripped off a second shot toward me. Fortunately, he missed, but he did manage to drive me back outside again.

A lot of good my appearance had done! More shots rang inside the sawmill. Somewhere in there,

Fairweather was trying to hold his own, and still wondering why I wasn't there to help.

I had to go back in, and was about to do so when more rifle fire erupted, this time from behind me. A bullet thunked into the wall above me and passed inside the sawmill. Remembering the two riders I had seen, I wheeled and ducked at the same time, coming down on the backs of my heels with my shoulders against the plank wall.

"No, Billy, no!" a youthful voice cried. "That's Mr. Brand!"

I saw the one who had shot at me—a lanky fellow in an oversized coat and straw hat. He was standing in an odd-looking, bow-legged half squat beside his horse, holding a smoking Henry rifle almost like mine. I caught the glitter of a tin badge on his black coat.

"She went and got the constable anyway!" I said out loud to myself. I recognized the youth with the lawman to be Fairweather's oldest son; he must have served as his mother's messenger boy.

So confused was the situation now that I didn't even have time to consider the implications of this new development. I reentered the sawmill to again attempt the relief of Robert Fairweather and the rescue of Leviticus Lee.

This time the tall man with the Remington was not at his previous post. In fact, I could see him nowhere. Once inside, I headed straight for Lee, who was yelling and writhing for freedom. Pulling a pocketknife from my coat, I said, "Hold still—let me cut you loose!"

Then the bald man popped up behind his woodpile, pistol in hand, and fired almost point-blank at me. The shot passed so close to my head that it clipped off some hair. I yelled and fired my Henry, and the bullet buried itself in the wood.

Immediately I vaulted over the woodpile, for I knew I had to rid myself of the bald man's threat before I could hope to free Lee. From across the sawmill Fairweather's yell, another cry for help, came ringing; I was encouraged to know he was still alive.

I landed on top of the bald man and drove my knee into his belly. He let out an "Oooof!" and tried to point his pistol into my face, but I deflected it, then hit him in the head with the stock of my Henry. It knocked him silly, but not out cold.

Just then I was aware of a shadow looming up behind me. It was the tall man with the Remington. He aimed and would have fired, but suddenly he spasmed and fell, simultaneous with the sound of a shot from the far end of the mill.

"I got him!" Robert Fairweather shouted.

Then began a quick succession of events that I would go through in my mind a million times thereafter, looking for whatever would have stopped it from happening, and never being able to find it. It was the confusion that caused it; that's the best all these years of assessment have been able to come up with. Confusion, and the speed of human reaction, and the inability of the mind to keep control of behavior once it begins running full-steam.

Here's the progression: I struck the bald man a second, lighter blow, designed to render him unconscious, but not kill him. Then Leviticus Lee sent up a holler, a warning, telling me to look out behind. I stood, wheeling around, as a figure came through the door. As I leveled my Henry, I saw two things—first, that the man at the door was the constable, and second, that Robert Fairweather had come out of his place of hiding at the far end of the stable and showed himself abruptly.

I remember seeing the constable raising his rifle, hearing myself yell out the word "No!" as loudly as I could, and then seeing and hearing the explosion of the constable's shot. At the other end of the building, Robert Fairweather took the slug right through the chest and jerked back and down like a dog hitting the end of its leash on a dead run. I yelled another no, then saw the constable's face go white. He dropped his rifle, recognizing who he had just shot. God help us, I thought, he's hardly more than a boy himself. A boy with a tin badge and a trigger finger that reacted before his mind could stop it.

The young constable collapsed to his knees, burying his face in his hands and crying in horror, "Oh, God forgive me, God forgive me, I've kilt Bob Fairweather!" At the same time, the Fairweather boy was running toward the collapsed heap that was his father, and then he was kneeling beside him, feeling his bloody chest, and at last crying himself as he slumped over and put his arms around the body as if he could squeeze the life back into it.

I knew then that Robert Fairweather was dead, and the thought made me sick clear through to the center of my very being. I stood there, watching the constable cry, until at last an urging voice managed to cut through the fog inside my ears and I realized that Leviticus Lee was begging me to free him.

Moving like a human machine, I stepped across the woodpile and also across the body of the tall man with the Remington. He was dead too. I opened my jackknife and sawed through Leviticus Lee's bonds while the sounds of grief rose on both sides of us.

There's no need to break down bit by bit all that had happened to lead up to the tragedy, or every detail of what happened immediately afterward. I'll turn things backward and give the broad strokes of the latter first.

After the constable got hold of himself again, he went from sad to angry, and turned a lot of venom on me and Leviticus Lee, on the grounds, as best I could tell from his nonsensical raving, that our presence in this county was the reason all this had happened, and therefore we were to be held to blame.

So he put us under arrest and hauled us off. Lee was taken somewhere "safe," they told me, but wouldn't tell me where. As for me, I was taken to Farleytown and stuck into the constable's "jail," a shack with double-thick walls, bars on the single window, and a rusty old cell door that fit in behind the regular one. The constable had built the thing himself out of what had been a woodshed near his own house. It provided the only secure place in the county to hold prisoners, except, of course, for the real jail at the county seat.

I was in despair, as you could suppose, not only about the death of Robert Fairweather, but also over being locked up when it was so pressing to get the gold and buy back Minnie. I almost told the constable about Minnie's capture, but held back because I saw he was so distraught about what had happened at the sawmill that he would either not believe me or would do something crazy in response and get Minnie killed.

Besides, I was fairly sure I could get out of this so-called jail, if it came to that.

Now, back to the sawmill tragedy and what led to it. Some of what I relate here I learned immediately after the incidents; other information came later, and some is based on my best supposition.

The bald man I had struck behind the woodpile in the sawmill was Parker Cuthbert. He didn't look a thing like I had pictured him. As suspected, he had hired the other man, the lanky one with the pistol, to capture Lee from the Fairweather house. The lanky man, who I later learned went by the name Jimbo Rollins, was a small-time criminal from Texas who had come to Arkansas fleeing a robbery charge, and had taken up with Cuthbert as a drinking partner. Robert Fairweather's shot had struck him in the upper chest and killed him instantly.

My blows to Cuthbert had knocked him out, but did no further damage. He too was arrested because of the horrible thing he had done to Leviticus Lee, and was taken to Dr. Ruscher's house under hired guard—a couple of locals who agreed to watch him while he was laid up. Cuthbert came to with both his guards sound asleep, and simply walked out the door. After that he couldn't be found.

As I had surmised, Blanche Fairweather was responsible for the constable coming into the picture. She had sent her son to get him just as soon as Fairweather and I had ridden out; the boy and constable had then come together to the sawmill.

No one ever knew what had caused Robert Fairweather to enter the sawmill before he should have. I suppose he mistook one of Leviticus Lee's yells as my signal. Whatever the case, it was that mistake, more than any other factor, that led to the tragedy.

The death of Robert Fairweather grieved me deeply. I felt responsible, even though it wasn't directly my fault. I knew in my heart that the person most at fault wasn't me, or even the constable who had fired the shot. It was my own Minnie, whose unfaithfulness was what had led me to Arkansas in the first place.

I paced inside the little woodshed jail, feeling like a kettle on full boil with nobody to take it off the stove. The constable was nowhere around, as best I could tell. Hours passed, and the light faded. There wasn't so much as a candle inside my prison, nor even a bed.

At length I lay down on the dirt floor and dozed off. It was very dark when the outside door opened. There, on the other side of the inner barred door, stood the constable, holding a lighted lantern.

And beside him was Blanche Fairweather.

16

Her face looked like that of a dead woman. No tears, no expression, nothing but an ashen, barren expression. She stared at me in silence. The only sound was a quiet, choked weeping from the constable.

"Mrs. Fairweather," I said falteringly. "I'm sorry about what happened to your husband."

"Sorry," she repeated. "Sorry, you say." She closed her eyes. "I knew when I first saw you that tragedy would come upon my family. I don't know how I knew it, but I did."

"Mrs. Fairweather, it wasn't me who killed your husband," I said. The constable gave a louder sob, then lowered his head. He had made the cycle from grief to fury and back around to even deeper grief. His hands shook, making the lantern light tremble. I felt a great sympathy for him. He was just a young man, and he had made a mistake that he would never be able to put behind him. "It was an accidental death," I quickly went on. "Just an accident, caused by the confusion. There's really no one to blame."

The constable sat the lantern on the ground and began to cry in earnest, leaning against the frame of the door. For half a minute it was like that, the constable weeping, and Mrs. Fairweather and I standing, looking at each other without words.

At last the constable turned and lurched off into the darkness, thoroughly overcome. Mrs. Fairweather hadn't yet shed a tear.

"It was him who shot Mr. Fairweather," I said. "He didn't really mean to do it. He didn't know what was going on—he just reacted, that's all."

"You've destroyed my family," she said.

"It wasn't me, Mrs. Fairweather. It wasn't me."

"I don't care who pulled the trigger. If you hadn't come into my household, none of this would have happened."

"I know that, ma'am. I've been sitting here alone, going over and over that same thought in my mind. But none of this was intended. None of it."

"But the result is the same."

"Yes . . . yes."

"He's dead, Mr. Brand—my husband is dead. I'm left a widow, and my children have no father."

"I want to make it up to you, somehow. Want to do something . . ."

"Do something?" Now, the first tears welled in her eyes. "Do something? What will you do? Raise my Bob up from the dead? Return him to me like he was before?"

How could I answer that? I stood silent.

"You can do nothing, Mr. Brand. Nothing but pay the price for what you did." And she reached into the pocket of her jacket and produced a small pistol. Trembling, she lifted it and aimed it into my face.

"Mrs. Fairweather, what will you gain by pulling that trigger?"

"Satisfaction. Vengeance. Justice."

"No. Your children have already lost a father. You'll deprive them of a mother as well. It will be murder if you kill me. And it won't be justice. *I didn't kill your husband!*"

"You're responsible all the same! I hate you!"

"Then hate me. But I didn't kill him. You have to understand that."

"Oh, you think I should use this pistol on that poor constable? You think I should blame him because he was the one who pulled the trigger? Because I don't—you've said with your own lips that it wasn't really his fault. It was an accident, one that would have never happened if you hadn't come to us uninvited."

"I came uninvited because my companion needed help. But you may recall that we weren't uninvited for long. Mr. Fairweather made it clear he wanted us to stay."

"Yes—because of the gold lust you revived in him. You cause it. You and your foul old partner. That's why I despise you. That's why I want the pleasure of seeing you die just like Bob died."

I saw then the depth of her hatred for me, a hatred I never would fully comprehend. She was able to see the truth of the constable's innocence with surprising ease, but where I was concerned, her mind was closed and locked. All her thoughts about me were irrational and bitter.

"I don't think you should use that pistol on me or anyone else, ma'am," I said. "And I think you're right not to blame the constable. But you're wrong to blame me or Leviticus Lee. Your husband came with me to that sawmill because he was a merciful-hearted man. There was far more to the man than gold lust; I know that now. He didn't want my wife to be murdered over a pile of lost gold, or Leviticus Lee to suffer at the hands of an evil man like Cuthbert. Your husband wouldn't want you to do what you're wanting to do, Mrs. Fairweather. And if you do it, you'll profane his memory and destroy what remains of your life. And a lot remains—all those beautiful children who need you. Think about it, and put away the pistol."

She began to cry very hard. The pistol lowered. "I hate you, hate you," she said. "I'll always hate you!"

The constable reappeared. His face was streaked and red, but he was not crying now. He had seen what was going on, and knew his duty. "Mrs. Fairweather, let me have the pistol," he said. "Please, give it to me."

She let the gun fall. He knelt and picked it up. Blanche Fairweather sobbed, turned away and ran off. I heard her climbing aboard the wagon upon which she had come, heard her drive off in the direction of her house.

"She told me she had to see you," the constable told me. "That's why I brought her. I didn't know she had a gun. If I had, I never would have—"

"I know. It's all right."

"I'll never be able to forget what it was like to see him fall, to know that I killed him." He looked off in the direction Blanche Fairweather had gone. "She's wrong to blame you. It's me who's responsible for Bob's death."

"It wasn't your fault. You were trying to do the right thing. There's no one blaming you."

"I feel responsible."

"No more than I do. We all had a hand in this.

But none of us planned it. None of us wanted it to happen."

He looked at me wearily. Then, as if on impulse, he dug out a key, opened the inner barred door, swung it open with a creak, stepped back and waved his hand. "Get out," he said.

"What?"

"Get out. Your guns and things are yonder in my house, inside the back door. Take them and go. Your horse and saddle are yonder at my stock shed."

He was setting me free! I couldn't believe it.

"Thank you," I said. "I appreciate—"

"Shut up! Just shut up and go. Get out of this county and don't come back."

"I will get out." To myself I mentally added: *But not until I've gotten Minnie back again.*

He was still standing in the little shed door when I rode away. I breathed a prayer for him, than one for Minnie, and then another for myself.

I had told Blanche Fairweather that I would do something to make up for the death of her husband. And I had meant it. What that would be, I had no idea. Yet I had to try.

But only after Minnie was safe. How could I get her back? At this point I hadn't yet learned where they had put Leviticus Lee, and there was no time to waste on a cold search for him. Nor did I have any notion of where Paul Merrick had stashed Minnie, nor if she was even still alive. If Paul Merrick had learned of the incident at the old sawmill, he might have panicked and already gotten rid of her.

I knew of only one place that might hold the answers I needed. I would have to go to Bass Merrick and reveal to him what his son had done. Maybe he would know where Paul Merrick might have taken Minnie. Maybe he would know where they had put Leviticus Lee. Maybe he would know something, anything at all, to help me—if only he would. I remembered the riders who passed me in the night, the ones who very well might have been sent by Bass Merrick to follow me. I had no grounds to trust the man at all.

Nor had I any other options. If Bass Merrick wouldn't help me, then there was no one else who could.

I was on the darkest stretch of the dark road when Parker Cuthbert appeared before me. He had a bandage on his bald head and a pistol in his shaking hand. He ordered me to stop, dismount, and throw down my pistols. I didn't know where he had come from; at that point I had no knowledge of his placement in and escape from the home of Dr. Ruscher.

"I knew I'd find you," he said. I could smell the liquor on his breath from where I stood. "You know where it is? Do you?"

"If you're talking about that gold, no, I don't know."

"You're a liar. You're a partner of Leviticus Lee. You know! You got to know!"

"No. Put the gun away, Cuthbert. You've dug a deep enough hole for yourself as it is."

"I'll not see my gold taken off by a stranger. It's my gold—I've searched for it for many a year. I've even kilt for it."

"Pete Revett?"

"Yeah, Pete Revett. Pete Revett the liar. He and me, we were friends once. He told me about hiding the gold. But he wouldn't tell me where it was. Said it was to be his, and his alone. He wasn't no friend at all. So I made him talk, made him tell me where he hid it, and then I kilt him. But he lied to me. It wasn't where he said it was. He had lied." He waved the pistol threateningly. "You won't lie. You'll take me to that gold. I would have had it by now if you hadn't come messing in my affairs. Leviticus Lee would have sung it out in good time if you hadn't interfered. Now you can make up for the trouble you've caused. You can take me to that gold as good as he could have."

"I don't know where it is. I'm not lying."

He clicked the hammer of the pistol. "You know—and if you don't talk, I'll kill you."

"Then what? With me dead, there's nobody to lead you."

"So you admit it! You *do* know!"

What could I do? The man was drunk, crazed, obsessed. I had no doubt he really would kill me if I overly frustrated him. So I nodded. "All right. You win. I'll take you to the gold."

He laughed like a child about to be handed a pound box of chocolate. "Smart man, smart man you are," he said. "Step aside. I'm going to ride that horse of yours, and you're going to walk in front of me, straight to that gold. One false move, and I'll kill you."

"I can't take you to it now—it's too dark. We'd never be able to find it in the dark."

"We can sure give it a try, now, can't we! Step aside!"

I had not the slightest notion where to go, so I walked along the main road. "I don't like this," Cuthbert said after a few minutes. "Somebody'll see us here. Where you heading?"

"The gold is near the old sawmill," I said, pulling

the locale out of the blue. It was one of the few places I knew how to get to. "Tell me something, Cuthbert— was that you who shot at me when I was burying Leviticus Lee's hand?"

"I wouldn't have done it if you hadn't come after me. I was watching the house. I figured you had the gold and were going to hide it for a time."

"You want that gold mighty bad, don't you?"

"More than anything, friend, more than anything. Listen to me: If we're heading toward the sawmill, there's a back road we can take. It's a little longer, but there's less chance we'll be seen."

Longer sounded fine to me; it would give me more time to come up with some scheme to get myself out of this. I dug around for ways to stall. "Wait a minute—we'll have to have a shovel. And a light."

"Light? What, is the gold down in a cave or something?"

"That's right."

He stopped. "There ain't no caves within a mile of that sawmill. What are you trying to pull?"

He had caught me in my own lie, but I faltered only a half second. "No caves you know of, you mean. The entrance is covered. That's why we need the shovel."

"Well, then we'll steal one along the way. There's a house or two we'll be passing." Suddenly he turned. "Wait—did you hear something?"

Indeed I had—it sounded like riders on the road behind us. But I said, "I didn't hear anything."

"There's somebody back yonder! Get off the road! Get!"

It was one of those sudden inspirations. I lunged forward, dropped to my knees and slid right under the horse. Then I let out a big yell, lunged up, and butted hard against the horse's belly with my shoulders.

As I had hoped, the horse spooked and reared. I rolled out from beneath to avoid being hammered by the hoofs. Parker Cuthbert, completely unready for my unexpected maneuver, and none too steady anyway because of his drunken state, hooted in surprise and was bucked clean off the horse. He landed on his back on the road just as the riders we had heard, three of them, came around the bend and into view.

It was too dark to make out who they were right away. All I could see was that the lead rider had a long shotgun. He stopped his horse, looked over the dark scene as best he could, then aimed the shotgun down at Cuthbert.

"Parker! So I've come looking for a treasure guide and found only a maggot." It was Bass Merrick's unmistakable Australian voice.

"Mr. Merrick!" I said, stepping forward.

"Well, I'll be!" he said. "Is that you, Brand? It was you I came looking for. I was just on my way to the constable to see about bailing you out—I heard about the incident at the old sawmill, and your arrest. I'm glad to find you. I have need of you."

"Enoch? *Enoch!*"

It was Minnie's voice, coming from behind Merrick. For a moment I was too stunned to react, then I darted toward her. "Minnie! Thank God!"

Merrick lowered his shotgun and shoved the muzzle into my chest. It caught me hard; my feet kicked out from beneath me and I fell onto my rump with an undignified thud.

"Not so fast, Mr. Brand," he said. "Not so fast.

There'll be time for reunions later, after our business is done."

"But how did you find her?"

"I know my son's hiding places. It was easy for me to get her. And that's the point to be stressed: *I* got her, not you. If you want her back, you'll have to earn her."

I was dismayed. "How?"

"Same deal my son offered you, the only difference being that this time you're dealing with me, not my pipsqueak of a boy. He's a loser, that one. Always has been. But I confess that this time he had him a good notion."

"How did you find out what he had done?"

"Paul's no judge of men—it's one of his many flaws. One of his 'friends' who was in on his little plan decided that I might reward him for sharing the scheme with me. Thought I might want to take it over, you see. He was right. Me and my man Jim, here"—he indicated the rider with him—"we just rode out and fetched your woman there right from Paul's grasping fingers. Now she's my prisoner, and you're dealing with me."

"Where's Paul?"

"Ran off pouting, and no doubt halfway to Texas by now. But enough talk. Have we got ourselves a deal, Mr. Brand? Gold for me, wife for you?"

I was so sick of this, so weary and hopeless, that I felt I could have fallen down in the road and died without complaint, just to escape. But all I could do was agree.

Parker Cuthbert rose. "Wait, Merrick. This here's *my* prisoner, not yours. And that gold is rightly mine too! You'll not snatch it from me!"

"Parker, Parker, Parker—if only you had any notion how wearying a man you are!" Merrick replied. "Don't you know that all the time I've given you a house to live in and put up with your presence, it's been on the slim chance that you might find that gold? If you had, you think I would have let you keep it? You're a bloody fool. You always have been."

"I thought you didn't believe that gold exists any longer," I said.

Merrick laughed. "So I said. But one never knows, does one! The more I thought about it, the more wonderfully possible the whole thing began to seem again. There may well be Confederate gold hidden in these mountains after all." His voice lowered and became coldly threatening. "You'd bloody well better hope there is too, Mr. Brand, if you want your dear woman back there to be safely yours again."

I could hear Minnie crying back in the darkness. I wanted so badly to go to her.

"I'll find your gold, Mr. Merrick. I'll find it for you—and when I do, I hope you choke on it."

Merrick laughed loudly. He seemed to think it was a very fine joke indeed.

Right then Parker Cuthbert made his move. He had dropped his pistol when the horse bucked him, but now he dove for it and retrieved it. In one swift roll he raised the pistol in both hands and shot Merrick's partner through the neck. The man pitched backward off his horse and thudded to the dirt. Minnie screamed, and Merrick swore. Cuthbert's second shot was aimed for Merrick, and it hit. Merrick took the slug in the shoulder and almost fell from his own mount. Cuthbert's third shot would have ended the encounter in his favor if he hadn't veered too much to the right and missed Merrick by little more than a hand's breadth.

That gave Merrick time enough to aim and fire. The shotgun's roar was fiercely loud, and the buckshot hit Parker Cuthbert squarely in the midsection. No second blast was required; it was immediately clear that Parker Cuthbert would no longer be a threat to anyone.

I headed straight for Minnie, hoping to somehow get my hands on her and get us away from here. It was a hopeless notion from the outset. Bass Merrick swung up his shotgun and brought it down on my skull. I fell to the ground, gripping the back of my head, then rolled over onto my back with a groan. Minnie was screaming.

"Shut up!" Merrick barked at her. From his voice I could tell he was hurting. He aimed the shotgun at her and looked down at me. "Mr. Brand, I wouldn't advise you to try anything like that again.There's still a loaded barrel in this shotgun, and I'll not hesitate to make your pretty wife look not so pretty anymore. Do you understand me?"

I sat up, my head throbbing. "I understand."

"Good. Now, stand up. We're going back to my house to patch me up, and then you're going to set out on a gold-retrieval venture, Mr. Brand. And you'll succeed, without any tricks, without any law, and without any hitch, or the lovely missus here will be a dead woman."

17

We made our way back to Bass Merrick's house. Merrick swore beneath his breath at the pain of his wound, and from his manner it was clear he was deeply disturbed by the killing of his underling, not to mention his own injury. And that was bad. Disturbed men react more than think, and often in irrational and dangerous ways.

And as Minnie reluctantly bandaged Merrick's wounded shoulder back at his house, the man seemed both irrational and dangerous to me. It scared me, more for Minnie's sake than my own. The way things had gone lately, I didn't expect anything but problems for myself. I was ready to handle whatever was tossed my way. But Minnie—that was different. If something should happen to her, that would be more than I could handle. Seeing the panic rising in Merrick, who until now had seemed the type to always be on top of his situation, was truly frightening.

"You're going to fetch that gold for me and bring it back here," he said, holding my own pistol on me with his good hand even as Minnie worked on his bloody shoulder. "I expect it in hand before sundown, or else I'll do what requires doing." I knew what that meant, and so did Minnie. Yet she didn't bawl out or collapse, as I might have expected. Perhaps the ordeals she had suffered had actually toughened her up a bit.

"Mr. Merrick, I won't lie to you. I don't know where that gold is. I never have known. Only Leviticus Lee knows."

If eyes could shoot lightning, his would have fried me thoroughly at that moment. "Mr. Brand, that had best be a bluff, for if it isn't, then you have no potential but to do me harm. And those who would do me harm are quickly swept away."

This was a dangerous man indeed. Even more dangerous than his son. "All right. I admit it was a bluff. I'll go get the gold."

What else could I have said? Anything else would have cost the life of my wife, and that of myself.

"Get on with you," Merrick said. "And if I catch even a whiff of law or treachery on your part, I'll make you a widower quicker than you can spit."

Alone in the night, I wondered what I could do. Where was Leviticus Lee? Given the torture inflicted on him in the old sawmill, was he even in condition to lead me to the gold, even if I could find him?

For that matter, would he be willing to do it? He had spent two decades of his life behind prison bars, living for the chance to gain the lost gold. He wouldn't be willing to turn it over to a man like Bass Merrick, simply to save the life of a man he really hardly knew—would he?

I had to hope he would, for without it there was

no hope at all. Bass Merrick had taken all my weapons. I wouldn't even be able to force Lee to help me, if such became necessary.

"Slow down and think," I said aloud to myself. "Where would they have taken Lee after the sawmill fight? Where?"

I had been hauled off and locked up, and Lee taken elsewhere. Realization struck, a realization so obvious it made me laugh. Lee was weak and injured after his ordeal at the mill. Where else would they take him but to Dr. Ruscher?

Encouraged, I increased my speed and rode toward Farleytown and the Fairweather store. It didn't strike me until I was in sight of the place that Dr. Ruscher only practiced there; his residence was elsewhere.

The window of his office in the store building was dark. Dismay swept over me. I had to find him, somehow.

My eyes turned to the saloons. Farleytown, though well-populated with drinking places, was no mining or railhead cattle town. The saloons didn't run all night. All that faced me was a row of dark buildings.

Dark . . . but not entirely. In the rear of one of the saloons a light burned. It was the same saloon, I recalled, that I had visited the day Paul Merrick was shooting the heads off buried chickens in the back.

I ran across the street and pounded the door so hard it rattled the adjacent window. Sure enough, there was somebody in the rear, and as he approached, I made him out to be the barkeep I had talked to before.

"What the devil are you doing?" he yelled

through the door. "I'm closed!" Over his shoulder I saw another person—a woman, seated at a table. The lamplight revealed a frilly, rather revealing dress. A soiled dove, no doubt, sharing the barkeep's liquor, and probably more.

"I need Dr. Ruscher," I said back through the door. "Where does he live?"

He opened the door and looked at me in a way that indicated he had just recalled my face. "Head up past the store—third house on the hill there, with a building behind it where he lays up sick folks sometimes. You hurt or something?"

"No. But I'm afraid somebody will be. Thanks, friend. No time to explain."

I took off on a lope toward the indicated house. I heard the saloon door close and lock, as the barkeep returned to his woman.

Dr. Ruscher adjusted his spectacles, lifted the lighted lamp he held, and looked at me with the bewilderment common to folks who have been roused from sleep at the oddest of hours. He ran fingers through his white hair and ushered me in.

"Mr. Brand, are you ill? And what are you doing running free—I thought you had been locked up."

"There's no time for me to explain myself right now, Doctor. I'm looking for Leviticus Lee. Is he here?"

"He was. He isn't now."

"Then where is he?"

"I don't know. I had him here. But this afternoon, when I went to check on him, he was gone. The constable had posted some guards over him and Parker Cuthbert, but after Cuthbert got free, the guards just walked away. I suppose they figured Mr. Lee was too weak to run off. They were wrong."

"No, no, no!" I burst out. "He can't be gone! I've got to find him! You have no idea where he went?"

Dr. Ruscher gave me a probing look. "Well, if I had to take a guess, I'd say he went after his gold."

"His gold . . ."

He said, "Come in. Let me show you something."

He led me to his kitchen. On the table were spread papers—mostly maps, showing the local region. I looked uncomprehendingly at them, then understood. "So you've looked for the Confederate gold too?"

"That's why I moved here upon my retirement, Mr. Brand. It was an interesting legend, and it attracted me. Oh, I've never been obsessed with it, like some; in fact, I've kept my interest in the legend entirely private. But it's been a good diversion for an old man. I've tromped around the mountains from time to time, trying to find it, with no more luck than anyone else. I suspect Mr. Lee may prove a more effective searcher."

"I think we will. He was one of the three who first hid it."

"Ah! I had thought that might be the case! Fascinating! That explains his ravings about the gold coins."

"You heard it too, obviously."

"Yes. It didn't take me long to figure out what gold coins he was talking about. You know, I had a feeling about that man, one of those unexplainable intuitions. I knew he had something to do with that gold. Fascinating! Just fascinating!"

"Dr. Ruscher, I've got no time to explain my situation right now. Suffice it to say that I've got to find

Leviticus Lee very quickly, and the gold too. Otherwise an innocent woman is going to die."

He frowned. "Die?" He seemed to withdraw. "Mr. Brand, I don't know what you're getting at, but I don't like the sound of it."

"I wish I could explain it more. All I can do is ask you to trust me, even though I know you've got no grounds for doing so. Dr. Ruscher, the woman who may die is my wife. Believe me, this is no fraud, no trick on my part to try to get something I've got no claim on." I waved at his maps. "Do you have any idea of what general area the gold is?"

"Nothing definite, but . . ." He paused, chewing his lip. "All right. Very well. I'll trust you. You have the look of honest desperation about you. Come, sit down. I'll show you what I can. But understand that this is nothing more than my best speculation, based on the study I've done concerning the legend, and my own explorations."

It was a meager lead, but all I had. I sat down, and he pulled up a chair beside me. Adjusting the lamp, he took up his maps and began to talk.

It was still dark when I left his house, but the first hints of dawn were lighting the eastern sky. I rode my weary horse into the mountains, following the route Dr. Ruscher had laid out. I had no real hope of finding the gold on my own. My hope was that Dr. Ruscher's information would lead me to the general area Leviticus Lee would have gone to recover his gold. With good fortune, I might be able to find him there—unless he had already come and gone.

I went as far in the dark as I could without risking the loss of my trail. This was unfamiliar terrain to me; it would be difficult under the best of circumstances to find my way. Finally I reached a point where I felt it prudent to wait for the full light of day before continuing. That time of waiting, though less than an hour in duration, seemed to last three times that long. I tried to relax, to let my weary body retrieve a little strength.

When the sun was finally up, I continued. Dr. Ruscher had scrawled a crude map for me, indicating various natural points of reference for me to look for. I was well-aware as I went on that I might be wasting my time. Dr. Ruscher had admitted that his study of the probable whereabouts of the gold had led him to conclusions at variance with those of most other treasure hunters. If the doctor's reasoning was faulty, I might be going farther away from Leviticus Lee, rather than nearer him.

Time seemed to have speeded up; as I made my way through valleys and beneath bluffs, up hills and down treacherous slopes, it seemed I was making progress far too slowly. Aching and tired, I forced the horse on, knowing it was as exhausted as I was. At last the land became too rough for riding to remain feasible. I abandoned and tied my horse and proceeded on foot.

Until finally I was there. A narrow valley opened before me, and leading into it the remains of an old and abandoned road. In a thicket I saw the rotting remnants of an old wagon. A military vehicle? Not enough remained for me to tell.

I descended into the valley. To my left rose a sheer limestone cliff, marked with cracks and crevices that might lead into caverns. At the base of the cliff I stopped, looking around.

I cupped my hands to my mouth. "Leviticus Lee!" I yelled as loudly as I could. "Leviticus Lee! Are you here?"

My call echoed away through the wild Ozark land. I raised the yell again. Still only silence in response.

Then, so close to me that I started in surprise, a voice replied, "Mr. Brand, is that you?"

"Leviticus!"

He was not thirty feet from me, lying in a bare spot behind a clump of scrubby brush. I could just make him out.

I circled the brush so quickly I almost fell atop him. He was on his back, looking as weak as death. In his hand he gripped a very rusty old Chicopee saber, like the Union cavalrymen had carried back in the war. And beneath his other arm was an equally rusted old box.

A strongbox. Marked with the letters C.S.A.

"Mr. Lee—you found it! You found the gold!"

"That I did, Mr. Brand. But I'm afraid I've nigh killed myself doing it."

And indeed he did look bad. Very bad. His face was pale, and I had seen healthier countenances than his in many a coffin.

I knelt beside him. "Are you hurt?"

"I was hurt before I started. Wasn't in any shape to do this. But I couldn't wait. I sneaked out of that doctor's place and came on out for the gold. Didn't know if I could find it, but I did. I looked for the big crevice, and dug. Sure enough, there was the saber. We had marked the spot with it." He weakly lifted the old blade. "An old Union saber—Pete Revett had come by it some way or another, and carried it. We buried it beneath an overhanging rock to mark the place. Once I found the saber, finding the gold was easy. Or as easy as any job can be for a man freshly deprived of one of his paws."

I examined the stump. It was blackened and ugly, and stank. Parker Cuthbert's abuse of the wound during Lee's ordeal at the sawmill had obviously badly damaged the arm. "Mr. Lee, this is bad. Real bad. We got to get you back to Dr. Ruscher, or I'm afraid this will poison you to death."

"It might. Wouldn't that be something! To find the gold, and then die."

"I've got a horse not far away. We'll get you on it and take you back. And then—" I cut off, dreading what I had to say. "And then I have to take that gold from you, Mr. Lee. Not for myself. For Minnie's life."

"Take my gold? You think you can . . . what do you mean . . ." He stammered into silence, and looked at me like I was Judas himself.

"Please, hear me out. Then you'll understand."

He lifted the saber and thrust it at me, driving me back. Weakly he stood. "You want my gold, and you'll have to fight me for it. Fight me clean to the death!"

"Listen to me. Just listen. That's all I ask right now. Just hear me out."

He was trembling very badly. The saber drooped to the ground, and he collapsed onto his rump. "All right, start talking. I don't appear in much shape to fight anyhow."

I told him the story, as best I could, from start to finish. He took it in without comment. Then he stood again, leaning on the saber like a cane. He looked down at the strongbox, sighed, and said: "Take it, then. Give it to Merrick, and buy back your woman."

"You mean that?"

"I mean it."

I could do nothing but stare at him. And I'm not ashamed to say that the tears rose in my eyes and spilled out.

"God bless you, Leviticus Lee," I said. "You're a saint. A saint, as sure as the world."

He shook his head. "No," he said. "Not a saint. Just a fool, that's all. Just an old fool with a heart that's even softer than his head."

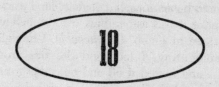

18

"We'll go back together," I told him. "You need to be looked at by Dr. Ruscher."

"No," he said. "I won't go back there. Too dangerous for me. When I sneaked off, I was still officially under the custody of the constable, and I can't afford an escape accusation. No sir. I'll stay here."

"You're in rough shape, Mr. Lee."

"I'll make it. Get on with you—get that gold to Bass Merrick and get your woman back before my old heart hardens up and makes me change my mind."

Any other time I would have argued with him harder, because he clearly did need medical attention. But my mind was full of Minnie right now; all I could afford to care about what getting her back. So I took the strongbox, thanked Leviticus Lee again, and returned to my horse.

With some cord from my saddlebags I strapped the strongbox onto the saddle behind me. Riding back through the rugged countryside toward the Merrick house, I thought how fine a man Leviticus Lee was, how remarkable it was that he was so willing to give up the gold that he had centered his life around, all to help me regain my captured wife. It was a sacrifice greater than many would have been willing to make. That a rough old former convict like Leviticus Lee would make it was astounding, even unbelievable.

I reined to a stop. *Unbelievable*, I thought again.

Dismounting, I loosened the ties around the strongbox and hefted it off and onto the ground. The lock was already broken away; Lee probably had done that. Kneeling, I took hold of the lid, closed my eyes, then opened the strongbox. Then I sat there, fearing to open my eyes again, for I knew what I would see was a box filled with stones or dirt.

I willed my eyes open, and what I saw took my breath. Gold coins, gleaming in the sun, and piled to the top of the strongbox. For a full minute I could do nothing but stare.

"Leviticus Lee, you really did it after all!" I said aloud. "You really are a saint—you really are!"

There was something different about the Merrick house, some vague change in the atmosphere that gave warning to my instincts as soon as I arrived. How I wished I had a weapon! I would have even welcomed the feel in my hand of that rusty old saber of Leviticus Lee's.

Dismounting in the yard, I took the strongbox and walked with it in hand up to the front door. As I was about to call for entrance, I noticed the door was slightly ajar.

My instincts were still sounding an alarm. So rather than call, I carefully pushed open the door and peered inside.

"Mr. Merrick? Mr. Merrick—I'm here. Where are you?"

No voice answered, but I heard a slight scuffling movement in the room beyond. I entered warily.

"Mr. Merrick, is that you?"

Then I rounded the sofa and saw him.

Bass Merrick lay on his back on the floor, staring up at the ceiling above him. But he saw nothing. He was dead, his chest bloody and punctured by at least three shots.

I dropped the strongbox in surprise and gaped at the ugly corpse for a few moments. Then panic began to rise. "Minnie? *Minnie!* Where are you?"

"She's right here, Mr. Brand."

I pivoted. Paul Merrick stood in the doorway to the next room. His left arm was around Minnie, and his right hand held a pistol that was aimed at her head.

"Minnie—are you all right? Has he hurt you?"

"She's as fine as fine can be," Paul Merrick replied. "And if that strongbox contains what I hope it does, she'll continue to be fine. If it doesn't, she'll be joining my dear father in the great world beyond, and you will too."

"Did you do this?" I asked, pointing at Bass Merrick's corpse.

"He deserved it," Paul Merrick said. "He humiliated me one time too many. This was my scheme, my plan, and he took it away from me. Took over my plan, and took your wife for his own hostage. I started off toward Texas, figuring that this time I'd never come back. But I had to come back and settle my grievances once and for all. I couldn't stand the thought of letting him get that gold. That gold will be mine alone. *Mine.*"

"Well, I've got it," I said, nudging the strongbox with my toe. "It's all there, and it's yours. Just give me my wife."

"All in good time," he said. "Open that box. I want to see it."

I knelt and opened the lid. Paul Merrick's eyes widened at the sight of the coins, and he smiled broadly, hungrily, and swore in awe at the sight. And indeed it was a sight worth seeing, a sight to rouse a fierce, ravenous greed in any man. But at that moment I was immune to the lure. All I wanted was my woman.

"You've got your gold. Now give me my wife," I said, standing.

He shoved her toward me without even glancing away from the box. I took her in my arms, hugged her to myself, whispered her name in her ear. I had never felt a feeling of relief and utter devotion to match the one running through me right then.

Paul Merrick knelt beside the box, chuckling to himself, his eyes as bright as flame. He looked at the coins a moment, then dug his fingers into them . . .

And the flame of his eye died. He drew in a sharp breath, pulled out a handful of the box's contents, stared at it, then with a curse threw it all down. What he had held was a few gold coins, and much more loose gravel.

Leviticus Lee had betrayed me. He had emptied the strongbox, filled it with gravel, and covered the gravel with a thin layer of gold coins. The vast majority of the gold wasn't here at all.

So that was why he hadn't come back with me! Even now, he was surely making his escape as fast as he could, taking the bulk of the Confederate gold with him.

It was the most disillusioning experience in my life. Leviticus Lee was no saint. He was a traitor, a scoundrel, a man willing to see me and my wife killed, just as long as he could get his gold.

Paul Merrick rose, leveling his pistol. "You thought you could betray me, did you? Where's the rest of it, Mr. Brand? Where's my gold?"

"I don't have it, I swear. Leviticus Lee has it, up in the mountains where he found it. I didn't know about this, Merrick. I swear to you I didn't know. He betrayed me too."

"You're a bloody liar, Brand! I ought to kill you and your trollop right now!"

My mind worked quickly, searching for a way out. "No," I said. "You kill us, and you'll never find the rest of the gold. Let Minnie go. I'll take you to where I found Lee. He's in bad condition—he can't have gotten far. We'll get the rest of the gold. But please, just let Minnie go."

He considered my words, then nodded tersely. "All right. We'll do it—but your wife comes along with us, and if anything goes wrong, anything at all, she'll be the first to die. You keep that in mind, Mr. Brand."

He herded us before him like sheep before a mounted shepherd. He had traded his pistol for his father's shotgun, so that he could easily hit us should we try to flee.

Minnie was pale but calm; I was proud of her. She wasn't the emotional and rather weak girl she had been before. She was stronger, more in control of herself. I wouldn't have willingly put her through the ordeals she had suffered for anything in the world, but I was glad to see the maturing effect they had wrought on her.

Life with Minnie might be better and happier now—if we survived this day to have a life together at all.

It seemed to take an eternity to make it back to the place I had left Leviticus Lee, and all the time I was conscious of the escape opportunity Lee was enjoying, and wondering how far he had gone. He might not have been as weak as he seemed to be; it might have all been pretense and fraud.

I was dismayed, but not surprised, to find no trace of Lee when we reached the clearing. Stopping, I looked around helplessly. I was exhausted, out of tricks, out of defenses. Leviticus Lee had left Minnie and me in a hopeless state, and I had no question about Paul Merrick would murder us as mercilessly as he had murdered his own father.

"He's gone?" Merrick asked.

I nodded.

Merrick shook his head. "I don't believe you."

"Look around. You can see for yourself that he isn't here."

"He never was here—that's my guess. It's you who found the gold, and you who are holding it out on me. You can put your hand on it if you want. You're just hoping I'll give up and turn tail." He lifted the shotgun. "Well, you're wrong."

Sometimes, when all hope is gone, defiance rises in its place. That happened to me. I stepped forward two paces. "If you're going to kill me, then do it. But let Minnie go."

"You really love that woman, don't you, Brand?"

"Yes. Let her go. She's had no hand in any of this."

He smiled, shook his head. "No. No. I can't let either one of you go, can I? After all, you both know I killed my father."

He was right. I felt a chill. Why hadn't I realized already that, gold or no gold, Paul Merrick couldn't let us live? We could implicate him for murder.

"What's your plan, Merrick? To blame your father's death on me?"

"Precisely, Mr. Brand. You came to rob my father, to extort from him, to bribe him—any old tale will do—and you grew violent and killed him. I pursued you into the hills and brought you down. A good and dramatic ending to the story of Bass Merrick's life, don't you think?"

"Don't kill us," I said. "I do know where the gold is. Let us live, and you can have it—and our silence." Such a pledge, I knew, could never save us, but maybe it would buy us time.

"Now you're cooperating! Good man! All right, take me to it."

I glanced around, as if looking for a sign or landmark, but in fact looking for anything at all that might help me gain the upper hand. By chance I spotted a flat stone slab that sat at a slight angle against the cliff base. Behind it was the dark opening of a cavern. Looking at the dirt around the opening, I saw Leviticus Lee's footmarks. This must have been the very place the gold had been hidden!

"It's in here," I said, and headed over to the cavern.

Paul Merrick brought Minnie with him. I squeezed between the slab and the cliff, and into the hole. Minnie came next. Merrick remained outside, peering in through the gap.

"You have a candle, or lamp?"

"No," I said. "I had a candle when I first came in for the gold, but it's burned away now. I got no matches, so unless you have some, we'll have to feel our way along to the gold."

He was hesitant. "This is a trick."

"No trick."

He shook his head. "Send the woman out again. You go and get the gold alone. If you don't come out with it, she dies."

I could have almost broken down and cried. In the darkness there would have been hope of me overcoming Merrick and getting the shotgun away from him. Now the situation was as hopeless as before—even more so, because Minnie's life now depended on me coming out of the cave with a cache of gold coins, when in fact no such cache existed.

"All right," I said. "All right."

With no other options before me, I edged back into the dark cavern, my back against the wall, my palms flat against the damp, dank stone. When I was several yards in, I felt in my pocket and found my box of matches. I had lied to Merrick about not having any.

I struck a match and held it up, then examined the floor. Sure enough, there were tracks here, both coming and going, matching Leviticus Lee's boots, and a drip of two of candle wax along the way. Additionally, there was a long, continuous furrow that might have been made by the corner of a strongbox if it was being dragged out—and a one-handed man would have had little option but to drag it.

Encouraged, I went forward, lighting my way with matches. At length I reached a sort of room with a natural stone shelf on one side, and by match light found the stub of a candle. Leviticus Lee must have left it. With my next-to-the-last match I lit the candle and looked around.

It was easy to tell where the strongbox had sat. There were plenty of tracks on the cave floor, and depressions left where Leviticus Lee had knelt. I could picture the scene: Lee kneeling in the golden light of his candle before this stone altar upon which sat the thing that mattered more to him than anything in the world—even more than the lives of innocent people.

I vowed to myself that if Minnie was killed or hurt, and I survived, I would track down Leviticus Lee and make him pay for what he had done.

Well, I had found the room, but what good did it do me? There was no gold here to be taken out to Paul Merrick. I searched for a scheme and came up cold.

And then the candle flame blew out as a cold wind brushed my face. In the darkness I dug for my last match—then realized the darkness wasn't complete, and further, that the wind had not blown in from the entrance that had led me here, but from the opposite direction.

There it was—a shaft of sunlight, filtering in around the next corner. This hidden cave had not one opening, but two.

My mind worked frantically, and I smiled. Not much of a chance, I thought. But at least a chance.

I headed for the newly discovered opening, praying it would be large enough to accommodate me, and far enough away from the place Paul Merrick was to keep him from seeing me.

19

Only with excruciating effort did I squeeze my way through the narrow secondary passage to the outside. I found myself on the far side of the hill from the cliff that overlooked the clearing where Merrick waited for me. Covered with slime and grease from the cavern, I began making my way over the hill and toward the bluff.

I paused long enough to find a large stone, about the size of a man's head. Picking it up, I hefted it the rest of the distance.

When the edge of the bluff came into view, I put down the stone, dropped to my belly, and snaked over to look down. There, maybe twenty-five feet below, was Paul Merrick, standing at the end of the slab that mostly covered the cavern opening. He was alternating between looking into the opening and glancing back to make sure Minnie wasn't making a break for freedom. She was in the center of the clearing, sitting on the ground, a very sad and hopeless look on her face.

I crabbed back from the edge of the cliff and got my rock. This time I proceeded on foot, right to the edge. Looking over, I gauged the angle of drop, the speed of the fall, and so on. I intended for this stone to strike Paul Merrick right on the crown of his head, and with any luck, to crack his skull thoroughly.

If Minnie hadn't spotted me and let out a gasp just as I dropped the stone, I think it would have worked. As it was, Merrick reacted to her noise by shifting his head a little, and the stone didn't make a direct hit. Nevertheless, it bashed the back of his skull soundly, drove his face into the rock and made him drop the shotgun. He collapsed, blood streaming down over the back of his neck and his collar.

Summoning my courage, I sat on the edge of the cliff, swung my feet over and pushed off. It was a long, long drop, seeming more like a hundred feet than the twenty or twenty-five it really was. I hit much harder than I had anticipated, my legs folding up beneath me like those hinged sectional yardsticks that store clerks carry in their pockets. The impact drove the breath from me, so that when I stood up and turned to face Merrick, I was completely unable to draw in air.

Fortunately, Merrick was in as bad or worse a shape than I was. The impact of the stone had stunned him, and he thrashed about like a drunken sailor freshly fallen overboard. I lurched toward him, hands extended to grab his throat. He tripped backward, landed on his rump, and his left hand found the shotgun he had dropped.

He raised it and fired; pellets fanned above my head. I was not even in shape to flinch or duck. I continued my advance, grabbing the end of the shotgun and yanking it out of his hand. It flipped through the air and landed in the clearing, near the place Minnie had been.

I say "had been" because she wasn't there anymore. She had taken off on a run as soon as I dropped over the cliff. Good for her. I hoped she would get far away, and survive no matter what became of me.

Paul Merrick and I struggled for the longest time at the base of the cliff. It was a primal struggle, a time of grit and sweat and blood and determination, and how long it lasted I can't say, but Minnie later swore it must have been an hour or more. We moved all across that clearing, each of us keeping half an eye on that shotgun, for one barrel remained loaded. At three points I almost got my hands on it, only to be dragged away each time by Paul Merrick.

I had just gotten in a fierce blow to his chin when he drove up his knee and caught me in the gut. I fell back to the edge of the rocky clearing, and when I tried to get up, I couldn't. And in the meantime, Merrick had staggered over and managed to get the shotgun.

That motivated me enough to make my next attempt at rising more successful. I tried to run, but didn't make it far before I fell again, onto my face this time. Merrick laughed as best his heaving lungs would allow, and came after me. When I rolled over, he was above me, his back toward a surrounding jumble of boulders, his trembling legs spread and slightly bent, and the shotgun wavering in his hands but managing to keep a sufficiently lethal aim right at my face.

"Mr. Brand, it's time for your last good-bye," Paul Merrick said.

I closed my eyes and prepared for the blast, but instead all I heard was a strange, choked cry. When I looked up, Paul Merrick was still standing there, staring down at his chest, from which a long, pointed, rust-colored object was protruding. For a couple of seconds I was confused, then I recognized it as the point and eight additional inches of the saber that Leviticus Lee had dug up. Paul Merrick made a few more choking sounds, then wheeled so that his back was toward me. The saber was still in him; now it was the handle and base of the long blade that was visible to me.

Paul Merrick had been run through, and the man who had done it was Leviticus Lee. He had emerged from the rocks behind Merrick as he was about to kill me. Had Lee had a hook in place of his missing hand, it would have been like a scene from some boys' novel of pirate adventure on the high seas.

Merrick screamed in fury, then lowered the shotgun and fired. Leviticus Lee took the blast in the midsection; the impact kicked him back against the rocks.

Merrick dropped the shotgun, gripped the blade that pierced him, and staggered off to the midst of the clearing. There he dropped to his knees. Twisting his head, he looked at me with a wild glare, like a man fresh-roused from sleep, moved his lips as if to say something that just wouldn't come out, and then fell straight forward, digging his right ear, and the tip of the saber, into the dirt below him.

"Why'd you come back, Mr. Lee? Why?"

He was barely conscious, and the blood rising into his mouth made it hard for him to talk. "Had to ... felt guilty, you know ... about what I had done ..."

"You were coming back to help me?"

"Yes ... tried to leave ... with the gold ... conscience wouldn't let me. Durn conscience ... plagues a man, you know."

He closed his eyes and swallowed some blood. I told him not to talk anymore, but he did anyway. "I was too weak . . . to carry the gold all the way . . . to Merrick's. Buried it . . . back yonder . . . map to get you there—it's in my pocket."

From his bloodied coat pocket I withdrew an old envelope. On the back of it was a map scrawled and marked with an X, showing the path from the main road to the new resting place of the old Confederate treasure.

"Mr. Lee, I'm going to get Dr. Ruscher," I said. "You rest, and I'll be back with him quick as I can."

"Too late, too late, Mr. Brand." He was making the most terrible noises in his shattered chest. "Lay me . . . in the cave."

Tears rose and came down my face. I wiped them away and nodded. "All right, Mr. Lee."

"Thank you . . . Mr. Brand. The gold . . . it's yours. You get it . . . spend it for me—hear?"

"Don't die, Mr. Lee. Please don't die."

"Don't think . . . it's up to me now," he said.

I cradled his head in my arms until the last rattling breath passed from him. Then, with tears in my eyes, I dragged his battered old form into the cavern that had hidden his treasure for so many years, and laid him to rest on the rock shelf.

When I came again into the light, I was wishing I had known him in other circumstances, and better. He had swept into my life and out again, and my life wouldn't be the same again because of him, yet he remained to me mostly a stranger, and now always would.

I found Minnie hiding in the woods about a quarter mile from the clearing. I told her what had happened, and in silence we walked together back toward Farleytown. I could have taken Paul Merrick's horse, which was tied in the woods, but it didn't seen prudent to risk being seen on the horse of a man who would at some point be found in a remote clearing, with an old saber jammed all the way through him.

I took the envelope Leviticus Lee had given me and examined the crude map etched onto it. Minnie saw it and asked what it was, and I told her. Her eyes got big and she looked at me with wild joy.

"Then we can go get it! Enoch, we're rich!"

"No," I said. "That gold has cost too many lives. I don't want a single coin of it; if we had it, I swear I believe it would ruin us. There's another that gold rightly should go to, and I aim to see that it does."

She couldn't believe it. She fussed and cried and yelled like the Minnie I had always known, and when we reached the road she turned and stomped off, declaring she was leaving me and I shouldn't come after her, because she never wanted to see me again.

Yes, indeed, Minnie was still the woman I had known. If she had matured in her ordeals, it hadn't stuck.

I circled around Farleytown to avoid being seen. On a tree trunk hung a fading old campaign sign from a past county election; I yanked this down and folded it. Then I continued on until I got near the Fairweather place, at which point I went out onto the main road to the place where their drive circled back toward the house.

There I knelt and dug from my pocket the stub of a pencil. On the back of the campaign flyer I scrawled these words:

Mrs. Fairweather—
    I know there's nothing to take the place
of your husband, but I told you I would do

what I could, and so I have. The map stuck here was made by Leviticus Lee, and if you follow it you will find wealth aplenty to see you and your young ones through the rest of your days. I am sorry about all that has happened, but want you to know again that I did not kill your husband.

> Yours truly,
> Enoch Brand

P.S.—When you find the gold, I hope you will share some of it with Dr. Ruscher. He is deserving of it.

I folded the paper, wrote "Blanche Fairweather" on the top fold, and put away the pencil. By now a couple of the Fairweather dogs had come from the house and were sniffing around me. I grabbed one of them and tied the note to the hemp collar around its neck, using a strip tore from my coat lining. Then I set out down the road, and watched long enough to make sure the dog headed back to the house.

I really hoped that Blanche Fairweather would go claim the Confederate gold. Perhaps, by letting the gold go to a good use like the care of a fatherless family, some atonement would be made for all the sorrow the cursed treasure had brought to so many.

Just then I heard a noise above me in the trees, then a voice: "Gold coins! Pretty gold coins!"

I looked up at the familiar creature in the branches. "That's right, Bird," I said. "Pretty gold coins."

Then I set off, heading down the road to overtake my still-straying wife before she got all the way to the next county.

If you enjoyed *Confederate Gold* by Cameron Judd, be sure to look for his next novel for Bantam,

BRAZOS

Here is an exciting preview of this new western novel, available in February 1994, wherever Bantam Domain titles are sold.

Turn the page for a sample of *Brazos* by Cameron Judd.

1

The first man stood alone in the late winter dusk. Before him were two graves that still bore the indentations of the shovels that had dug and filled them many days before.

The graves were marked with wood crosses and lay near the place the house had stood. The house itself was now nothing but a pile of thoroughly burned, stinking timber. The fire must have raged every bit as hot as the folks in nearby Cade had declared, for the ground for several yards all around was blackened even yet, the chimney had crumbled to a rubble heap from the heat, and two nearby outbuildings had also burned to the ground. The little cookhouse and adjacent bunkhouse stood on the other side of a narrow grove of trees, out of sight and far enough away that they had been spared destruction.

Hat in hand, the mackinawed man stood by Magart Broadmore's final resting place and wondered morbidly how anyone had managed to find any human remains worthy of burial after such a conflagration.

He was a tall man in his forties, broad-shouldered and long-legged. Unlike his smooth-pated father, who had balded in his twenties, he had managed so far to keep every bit of the thick shock of hair that curled behind his ears despite all his efforts to comb it straight. It was gray at the temples, but the rest remained black as nightshade. If not for his thoroughly weather-creased face, he might have passed for a man ten years younger than he was.

Usually he was calm and stoic. But today he was deeply shaken, and glad to be alone where no one could see the dampness and redness of his eyes. He had come to the Brazos country expecting to find a long-estranged sister. He had not come expecting to find her and her husband dead, and their ranch abandoned.

His moistened eyes shifted to the other grave, the one closest to the ruins of the house, the one marked F R. BROADMORE—b. 1842, d. 1875. His lip curled in distaste that approached hatred. He harbored no grief for this grave's occupant. Folly Broadmore had been a sorry soul in life, and death did nothing to make the thought of him any more tolerable. The man was born no good and had lived up to his heritage. Gambler, cheat, sometime swindler, full-time loser. That was Folly Broadmore.

Too bad they were already buried when I got here, the man thought. *I never would have let them bury Magart beside him. It ain't right that she has to lie beside a man like him, even if he was her husband.*

He turned away, eyes sweeping the rolling Brazos country. He dug a hand under his coat and into his pocket to fetch out his tobacco and papers. Within a few seconds he had rolled a perfect cigarette, or quirly, as he would have called it. Snapping a phosphorus-and-sulfur match off the matchblock in his pocket, he struck flame on his bootheel and lit the tobacco. The smoke of it was raw against his throat, but it soothed him.

The sun, swollen and orange, was nestling its lower edge against the western horizon. The wind rose higher, carrying the scent of river and town through the chill-sharpened air. The man sniffed. Funny thing, he mused, how that lousy town seemed to have its own distinct scent, like a living thing. He could pick it out from here, a full two miles away. It was a conglomerate smell of humans, horses, dogs, pigs, cattle, timber, chimney smoke, tobacco, whiskey, and all the thousand other things that went into the mix of the ugly little farrago that had grown up in the shadow of equally ugly Fort Cade.

The man tossed down the quirly and crushed it under his heel. Putting foot to strirrup, he swung into his gelding's saddle, and rode slowly by the light of the sunset back toward Cade. There was only one thing to do at a time like this: Get as drunk as possible, and stay that way as long as he could.

The second man wasn't as tall as the first, but every bit as lean, perhaps leaner. His hair was wispy, thinning on the crown of his head, and its color was that of wet sand. His skin was fair; more freckled and windburnt than tan.

He was crouched in the brush beside a curving stream that snaked between two low hills wooded with oak. Above him hung an orange and violet sunset. He held a battered carbine, already levered and cocked, and his heart thumped like a hammer. A little rivulet of blood stained his calf, coming from a superficial bullet wound suffered while he rode in a dead heat away from the three horsemen who had pursued him.

He hadn't recognized any of the three and hoped they hadn't recognized him. Who were they? Ranchers, cowboys ... or range detectives? He hoped not the latter, though the possibility was there. Local ranchers were getting weary of losing stock, and drastic measures, such as hired range guards, could not be too long in coming.

He shifted his posture and winced at the pain of his wound. Glancing at it, he wondered how deep it was. The pain of it was certainly noticeable, though there was not the dull throb of a deep puncture. It had been a grazing shot, nothing more. But he would have to get rid of these bloodied trousers, for a bloodstained and bullet-torn fabric would generate some uncomfortable questions back in Cade.

He crouched where he was for the next half-hour. Finally, when it was almost fully dark, he stood, grinning broadly. No pursuers had appeared; they must have gone past on the far side of the rise. He spoke to the black horse that searched for early forage behind him, down by the water and out of sight of any potential watchers from the rolling countryside beyond the oak stand. "Horse, I think we shook 'em."

He examined his wound; as he had thought, it was superficial. It had already quit bleeding on its own. The sting was gone now, leaving only a slight ache. Limping a little, he got the horse, mounted and rode out of the thicket, heading east toward his big ranch house.

Cheerful though he was at evading capture, the experience had sobered him. He would have to be more careful in the future. He had too much going for him here in Cade to be careless. Too many plans, too many ambitions, too much to lose—and lose it all he would, if ever he was pegged as a stock thief. From here on out, he decided, he would have to leave the actual act of stock theft to his associates in crime. From now on he would play his role strictly in the background, carefully hiding the vital secret of his involvement. This would be especially important after the election was over and he was firmly ensconced in the county sheriff's office over in Cade.

On his way back to his big stone house, the man rode across the Broadmore spread. He paused there, looking toward the black rubbleheap of the house. There was just enough light for him to make out the two crosses on the graves. He eyed them a moment, then rode on.

2

Two days later

Paco the Mex saw his beloved one drawing near. He
stirred where he lay, eyes closed, and smile. "Bellina,"
he whispered worshipfully. Bellina of the mysterious
darkness, Bellina of eyes and hair black as midnight,
Bellina of brown skin as cool to Paco's touch as the bottle
of whiskey that had given her the only reality she now
possessed.

"Paco ... *hermoso, fuerte* ..." Her voice was musical
and sweet, soothing to hear, even if only in his imagination.

Only when Paco was drunk did Bellina come to
him, and as far as he was concerned that provided the
best of many good reasons to get drunk as frequently as
possible. When he was sober, all life had to offer was the
squalor of this town: its dirt, poverty, heat, danger, and a
populace that looked down on him and made him look
down on himself. When he was drunk, things were better. Intoxication gave Paco the only two luxuries he had
known for many years: escape from ugly reality, and
Bellina, a lover made of memories and dreams.

Yet now, as Bellina reached out to caress him, her
touch was not a phantom's, but solid, human. A thrill
shivered through Paco. She was real! She was alive!
"Bellina, bella Bellina ..." He smiled broadly, reaching
out to her as he opened his eyes.

Paco's body jerked upward and suddenly he was looking into a stubbled male anglo face that was certainly not that of his imagined lover. The Mexican's lip curled back over a wide gap where front teeth had been in the days when he had been young and handsome and had loved a real-life Bellina, now many years in her grave. A gargling, panicked sound bubbled up from his throat.

"Bellina, eh?" the anglo said. His eyes were red and his breath heavy with whiskey. Paco was face-upwards, his liquor-weakened legs, all one-and-a-half of them, sprawled out. He had removed his whittled pegleg for comfort's sake before settling down to drink; now it lay beside him. His torso was pulled half-upright as the anglo held him by the collar of his ragged coat. "I'm a long way from being any Bellina, amigo. You're the one they call Paco the Mex?"

"*Si, si*—I am Paco. *Misericordia*, señor, mercy . . ."

"They tell me you're a cheap thief and beggar, Paco. That right?"

"*No, señor—no lo quiera Dios!* I am no thief. I beg you, let me go!"

"You're a pitiful excuse even for what you are, Paco. The smell of you alone is enough to make a man sick. You think any sweet Bellina would have anything to do with a skunk like you? Do you?"

"No, *señor*. No. I am a wretch, *señor*. *Por favor*, don't hurt me!"

"Hurt you? Why would I want to hurt you? Of course, if you decide to be uncooperative . . ."

"What do you want of me, *señor*?"

"I want you to tell me what you know about the death of Magart Broadmore."

Paco suddenly recognized the man who held him. His tongue swiped out; his eyes grew wide, making the brown-black pupils stand out against the background of the surrounding bloodshot whites. "Keller!" he said. "You are Keller!"

"That's right, Paco. I am Keller, and before she married, Magart Broadmore was named Keller too. She was my sister, Paco. I came here to find her, and what I found instead was her grave. Now I hear whispers in the saloons that you know more about how she died than what the local rag wrote."

"No! I know nothing!"

"Only a dead man knows nothing, Paco, and if you don't talk, dead you'll be. Tell me what you know about Magart Broadmore's death!"

"The fire, she died in a fire, she and her husband!"

Keller swore and shook the Mexican. "Tell me what I don't already know! Tell me the truth!"

"*Señor, por favor*, I know nothing more! I swear it before God, before the blessed Virgin! I know nothing!"

"That's not what I hear, Paco. They tell me you talk too much when you're durnk. They tell me you say it wasn't the accident it was claimed to be!"

"Please, *Señor* Keller, believe me—if I knew anything, I would tell you!"

Keller's face became hard and ugly. He was driven by liquor and fury, a state he was unaccustomed to, and therefore could hardly control. His lips tightened to a line. "You're a liar, Paco. A liar and a scoundrel. And letting you keep on breathing is a waste of good air."

Keller drew his pistol and thrust it into Paco's face. He was thumbing back the hammer when he suddenly froze, realizing the horrible thing he was about to do. *God help me, have I sunk so low as to murder a man in an alley?*

Paco wrenched free and screamed in terror as he fell back, spreading his arms behind him to catch himself. In so doing, he chanced to put his fingers around the pegleg. He grabbed it, swung it up, and clubbed Keller soundly in the side of the head. The pistol went off in Keller's hand, splattering a harsh powderburn across the left side of Paco's face but sending the slug into the ground beside him.

The Mexican hit Keller again, knocking him aside, then leaped to his single leg. Still yelling frightfully, he began hopping away, pegleg in hand. He bounced off around the corner of the stable behind which the encounter had occurred. Keller was on his knees, grimacing and slightly dizzy from being clouted. He picked up his pistol and held it limply. "God, I almost murdered a man!" he murmured to himself. He gingerly touched his head where Paco had struck him and found blood on his fingers when he took them away.

Keller stood waveringly, pistol dangling in hand, and heard footfalls on the side of the building opposite where Paco had just run. He turned as two wide-eyed men with identical deputy badges and almost identical faces emerged to face him. One already had his pistol drawn; the other drew his as soon as he saw Jed standing there with weapon in hand.

"Drop that pistol! Drop it!" the first man ordered. Keller had seen these lawmen before and knew they were the Polk twins, Homer and Haman, lookalike brothers who helped the county sheriff ride herd on the town of Cade and its surrounding environs. Which was Homer and which was Haman, he didn't know.

Keller stooped and laid the pistol on the ground. Standing, he lifted his hands. A think trickle of blood edged down under his collar.

Who were you shooting at?" the lead Polk demanded, pistol trained on Keller.

"Nobody," Keller said. His anger had drained out, replaced by shame and desperation. He wanted badly to turn and run.

"That's a lie. I heard yelling."

"That was me," Keller said, groping for an out. "I saw a snake, yelled, and shot at it. Snakes scare me bad."

"I heard Paco the Mex's voice back here," the second Polk said. "And I don't think no snake clouted you in the skull."

"Look, men, I'm a longtime peace officer myself, and this looks to me like a situation you ought to just let drop," Keller said, flashing what he hoped was a disarming grin.

"I reckon you would think that way," the first Polk said. He squinted. "Hey, you're that Keller fellow, ain't you? Brother of poor old Magart Broadmore?"

"I am. How do you know me?"

Polk cleared his throat, looking ill at ease. "The sheriff said you were in town. I'm sorry about what happened to your sister, Mr. Keller. I feel sorry for you and all. But I can't let you go until we know what was going on back here."

Another man came around behind the Polks. "Haman, Paco the Mex just hopped all the way down the street with one side of his face burnt red, yelling he'd been shot at. He looked drunk, but he was hopping like a dang jackrabbit."

"So that *was* Paco I heard yelling back here!" Haman Polk declared. "You lied to us, Mr. Keller. Come on. Let's go see Sheriff Cooke."

"Wait a minute . . . did you say Cooke?"

"Yeah. Till Cooke. He says he knows you. Planned to look you up while you were in town. It looks like we'll be saving him the trouble. Now come on, get moving."

Keller walked all the way to the sheriff's office with Haman Polk's pistol trained on the small of his back, his hands uplifted to shoulder level, and a stunned expression on his face. Till Cooke was the law in Cade? He hadn't known that. It was the first good thing he had heard since arriving here.

Or maybe it wasn't so good. How would Till Cooke react to learning that a man he had trained in the ways of the law had fallen to the point of beating on peg-legged Mexicans in back alleys?

This one was going to be difficult to explain, especially to a stern law-and-order man like Till Cooke.

3

The next morning

Till Cooke had once stood five inches above six feet tall—an imposing height that had caused many a violence-prone drunk to take the better part of discretion once faced with the towering lawman. But the years had done their work on him, arching his spine and robbing almost three inches from his stature while adding them, plus many others, to his girth. Cooke's jowls had stretched and drooped, his hair had faded to white, and his once-erect shoulders had rounded off like weatherworn boulders.

He took a final pull on the cigar that had rested on his lip since breakfast. It had been lighted, allowed to go out, and relighted all morning, until now only an inch of it remained. Cooke flipped the butt into the belly of the stove in the corner of the office, stretched, and addressed Haman Polk, who was seated on the corner of the big paper-piled rolltop situated off-center in the office.

"So old Jed's got himself arrested, huh?"

Haman Polk used his official voice, deeper and cleaner-clipped than his usual slur. He and his brother were young men, recently hired, and still stood in awe of their seasoned superior. "Yes sir, Mr. Cooke. Somebody told him that Paco the Mex has been talking about the fire that killed his sister, and Keller got drunk and decided to try to scare Paco into talking. Keller swears he didn't intend to fire a shot. Says it was an accident."

"I see. Did Paco file a complaint against Keller?"

"Oh, no. He was so scared he denied it ever happened, once we started questioning him. But he was seen hopping scared down the street with a powderburn on his face, so we know it happened. Homer tracked him down. He was hiding behind the rain barrel in the alley beside the Big Dakota."

Till Cooke said, "I'm going back to talk to Keller."

"He's sleeping."

"Then I'll wake him up." He gave a snorting chuckle. "I expected to see Jed while he was in town, but I didn't expect it would be like this."

Jed Keller was on his back on the cell bunk, his hands behind his head. The cell's pillow had been ripped to pieces by a drunk who had occupied this cell the previous night and now was nothing but cloth and feathers all over the floor. Keller had been allowed to keep his hat, and it rested on his forehead, tipped down to shade his eyes. The only other occupant of the jail was in an adjoining cell separated from Keller's by a stone wall, and was also asleep.

Till Cooke left the cell door open and walked over to the bunk. The cell was chilly. He crossed his arms and studied the reclining prisoner. Keller moved a little, then reached up to push back the hat enough to let him see.

"Dog if it ain't really you after all, Till," Keller mumbled sleepily. "Just like them twins said. How you doing?"

"Tolerably well, Jed," the lawman said. "Keeping myself out of hot water, which is better than I can say for you."

Keller flipped the hat off onto the floor and sat up, groaning as morning-after discomforts hit him. He yawned and stretched very slowly. "I've stepped in it this time, I admit, and I'm ashamed. I was drunk. Wouldn't have done it otherwise." He froze in mid-stretch as he got his first good look at the sheriff. "Dang, Till, you're old!"

"I am, no denying. I ain't got a day younger since I seen you. Now, why don't you scoot over, and give a tired old man a chance to rest his backside, huh?"

The bunk creaked under the added weight. Till Cooke sighed, dug a new cigar from his vest pocket and bit the end off it. For the sake of his personal budget he allowed himself only two good cigars a day. If he needed smokes beyond that, he made do with the foul-smelling "short sixes" they sold for a penny in the saloons.

After he had fired up, he reached into his pocket and handed a cigar to Keller. It was one of his good ones.

"I'm sorry about Magart," Cooke said through the rich smoke. "It's a hard thing to lose kin."

"I didn't even know she was dead until I got here," Keller said. He chuckled ironically. "Funny, in a way. You come to make peace with your sister after too many years and find out she's dead and gone. Ain't that just the way things go!"

"Unfortunately it is." Another drag and puff. "Was it because of Magart you were pestering Paco the Mex?"

"Yeah. I heard he had been talking about a secret he knew, a secret concerning the Broadmore fire."

"Where'd you hear that?"

"A gent in a saloon. He said he Paco had tried to sell him the secret in exchange for a bottle. The fellow told him no sale."

"Likely that fellow was just one of Paco's many antagonists. He's sort of the village idiot, you know. Folks like to give him a hard time."

"So you don't think Paco really knew anything?"

"Generally speaking, Paco don't know beans from bullets. He's half crazy from drinking his life away, and makes up all kinds of stories, most as wild as weeds. Folks like to pick on him, just to make him squeal so they can have a good laugh. Life is hard for that poor old Mexican." Cooke's cigar sent him into a coughing fit. He hacked into his hand, cutting off conversation a few seconds. He cleared his throat and went on, now in a more somber tone. "Jed, I wish you hadn't have shot at Paco. It makes it look like you were sure 'nough wanting to kill him."

"It was an accident. He hit me with that wooden leg and made the pistol go off. Like I said, I wouldn't have done any of it if I hadn't been drunk."

"If you'd killed him, that would have been murder. And I would have seen you prosecuted—even if you were the best Missouri deputy I ever hired."

"I know. You'd hang your own father if he stole a horse, Till."

"Speaking of fathers, how's yours?"

"He's dead, Till."

"Mark is dead? I'm sorry to hear it. How long?"

"A month or so. It was a natural death. He was just old and wore out." Jed paused. "And he never forgave Magart for marrying Folly Broadmore. Took the anger to his grave. That's the main reason I decided to come look her up. A family ought not fight amongst itself. I wanted to patch up all the old wounds with her."

"Must have been quite a kick in the gut to get here and find out what had happened to her."

"Yeah." Keller looked sidewise at Till Cooke. Now that he was past the surprise of seeing how the years had weathered the man, he seemed more like the Till Cooke he had known when he was a neophyte deputy in Missouri and Cooke, then his boss, was still ranked among the toughest of the frontier lawman. "What do *you* know about that fire, Till?"

Cooke shrugged. "No more than anybody else. It started round the fireplace, as most do, and burned the house to the ground with Magart and Folly still inside. Both bodies were found. Now they're buried together in the yard. It was an accidental thing, as best anybody can tell. It's mighty sad; the Broadmore ranch was turning into a good spread."

"Was Folly good to Magart?"

"I won't lie to you, Jed. He wasn't. They say he treated her pretty rough."

Keller ground his teeth and to himself cursed Folly Broadmore's name.

"Let me give you some advice, Jed, not as sheriff to prisoner, but as one old friend to another. Go ahead and grieve for Magart, go ahead and hate Folly Broadmore for being what he was to her—but then put it aside and forget about it. You can't change a thing that's happened, and you can't let yourself get into such a state that you go around Cade pulling pistols on poor old Mexicans and such. You do any more of that, and I'll have to start interfering something fierce in your life."

"Hah! You've already interfered, it appears to me. You've got me locked up, ain't you?"

"Not anymore. You're free to go—but you heed my warning, hear? Let it go. She's dead, and nothing you can do will bring her back."

Jed Keller nodded, saying nothing.